S w e e t m e a t s

Travel brings new experiences and discoveries into everyone's lives. Vistas broaden as new landscapes unfold beneath our feet and new people are met.

We wanted to tell stories of adventurous spirits, changing perspectives, and expanding sexual horizons. These authors do not disappoint, as they tempt and excite with exploits and escapades that span the world. The joy of travel and the wonder of sex are brought beautifully together in five captivating tales.

A Sweetmeats Book

First published by Sweetmeats Press 2015
Copyright © Sweetmeats Press 2015

2 4 6 8 10 9 7 5 3 1

ISBN 978-1-909181-52-6

Typeset by Sweetmeats Press
Printed and bound in the U.S.A

Sweetmeats Press
27 Old Gloucester Street, London, WC1N 3XX, England, U. K.
www.sweetmeatspress.com

WANDERLUST

compiled by

KOJO BLACK

SWEETMEATS PRESS

*"Twenty years from now you will be more
disappointed by the things that you didn't do than
by the ones you did do. So throw off the bowlines.
Sail away from the safe harbor.
Catch the trade winds in your sails.
Explore. Dream. Discover."*

-Mark Twain

Contents

THE PASSENGER

ANNABETH LEONG

The Passenger

Suzanne Houston hadn't skulked into the parking lot of the town truck stop since the night before she'd been married. She came to it from the woods side not the highway, the way she always had when she was younger. She ducked and lurched through sprawling tangles of undergrowth, worried about spiders and chiggers and worse. Rotting leaves crunched under her feet, and slimy little touches along her bare legs made her limbs shiver and jerk. The earth beneath her smelled humid and carnal—or maybe that was her own body.

She wore no bra or panties under her dress. Thomas had thrown both her and her vibrator out of the house without giving her a chance to retrieve the undergarments she'd discarded before the night's epic masturbation session. He'd come home early from his night shift and caught her, still bleary from her orgasms, her clit half-numb after hours of intermittent vibration, her pussy so utterly wet it was frictionless, and shudders of electricity licking through her pelvis as nerves satiated beyond endurance attempted to continue functioning.

Instead of recognizing a good opportunity when he

saw one and taking out his cock to finish her off, Thomas had started screaming incoherently about slutty, whorish behavior and her supposed attempt to replace his penis with a piece of silicone. Suzanne pointed out sharply that she'd be more than happy if he wanted to introduce some real meat to the equation. After all, she'd only been begging him to for a *solid week and a half.*

Her retort had only made him angrier. Thomas yanked her vibrator's plug out of the wall, taking half the socket with it. Suzanne blinked and stumbled to her feet, her thigh muscles trembling and her knees gelatinous. She hadn't been in much shape to argue her case.

Hence the truck stop. She used to flirt with truckers as a way of flirting with leaving town. Sometimes, she'd even hitched a ride for a few dozen miles and maybe a blowjob, but Suzanne had always lost her nerve well before making it to the state line. When she married Thomas, she gave up the charade and accepted she'd never get out of Summerton.

Tonight, she'd gotten mad enough to toy with the thought again. Suzanne wanted a piece of pie and a greasy burger and a man who wouldn't mind seeing her play with her pussy. On the other hand, maybe she just needed a place to cool off where Thomas couldn't find her. He'd never think to look for her here.

She emerged from tree-shaded darkness into the outskirts of the parking lot, greeted by blinding neon and halogen lights. Her hands closed around the rotted wooden fence that stood between her and her destination. She tossed one leg over it, then the other, careful to avoid splinters but not cautious of whatever view she might flash.

Trucks hunkered in the lot's darker corners, chrome-colored and muscular. Through the truck stop diner's big plate-glass windows, she saw a couple of guys nursing cups of coffee. At this hour, most of the truckers had probably bedded down in their cabs. Suzanne sighed. To take her pick of the men, she'd have had to get here a lot earlier.

And she *would* have had her choice of the men, even dirty from the woods and wearing no makeup and smelling like cunt. Suzanne might be married, but she was still only 22. She was pretty, not stunning, with long black hair, dark eyes, olive-colored skin, and features that suggested a varied but indeterminate ethnic background. The key to her success with the opposite sex had always lain in a set of qualities that didn't show up in photographs. The sweet tang of her aroused pussy tended to rise around her whenever she talked with an interesting prospect. By the time she'd graduated from high school, she'd mastered the art of signaling sexual interest with a brush of her fingertips to the back of the other person's hand and the angle she held her head. And, of course, there was that vibrator Thomas hated so much. Her secret weapon. Fresh from a session of blowing her own mind, Suzanne usually oozed a cocky sexuality that men found irresistible.

She crept closer to the window and considered turning her charms on one of the truckers still inside. One of the men looked up as if sensing her there. He had a sharp, wolfish face framed by stringy black hair. Hollow cheeks made him look hard and worn, but he had the bone structure of a handsome man. His eyes widened when they met hers, then narrowed as if he thought he could trap her between his eyelids. The naked hunger of his scrutiny instigated her wetness anew. She knew she could walk in and take him without saying a word. If she dipped a finger in her pussy now, then went into the diner and held out her glistening hand to him, she knew he'd follow her anywhere she wanted to go. Maybe to the other side of the building, where she recalled a little staircase they could lean against, a good place to lift her skirt for a quick screw.

Like most of Suzanne's fantasies, this was easier said than done. She'd never cheated on Thomas, despite his accusations earlier that night. She wanted revenge, but didn't want to give up her moral high ground. She wanted adventure, but she'd never been brave enough to overcome the fear that stood in its way.

She slipped back into the shadows, and into another old habit.

Long ago, Suzanne discovered that in a town like Summerton, a lot of guys didn't lock the backs of their trucks. So sometimes at the truck stop, she'd check. Suzanne did that now. She tugged at handles and tested various sliding mechanisms until she found one that opened to her touch. Shorter than the others, this truck spoke to her of more precious cargo than most. In a parking lot full of 18-wheelers packed with wood or plastic or oranges, this little box truck stood out like a sore thumb.

Suzanne didn't climb in just yet. She slipped around the outside of the truck, drumming her fingers against the corrugated metal siding of the box. It bore no identifying marks, so it couldn't be a rented moving truck. She crept as close to the cab as she dared and peered in. Not seeing the driver, her mind immediately flashed to the wolf-faced man in the diner. Arousal followed. She liked the idea of getting caught in his truck.

She grinned. This sort of fantasy she could act on—one with avoidable consequences. She ran to the slightly open back and knocked on the aluminum. "Hello? Anyone in here?"

She heard no sound, but as she leaned her head into the dark space inside, she noticed a powerful, pungent aroma. It wasn't exactly the smell of pussy but it was in the family, salty like ocean water but with dark undertones. Swampy rather than beachy, maybe. The scent brought to mind poisonous plants, leaves of a nearly-black green, and treacherous footing, with god-knows-what hidden in the mud. Suzanne blinked and shook her head at herself. Given the hour, her brain was probably half-dreaming. That might explain the lurid imagery tumbling through it.

Still, she wanted to know where that smell really came from.

That settled it. Curiosity aroused along with the rest of her, Suzanne slid her slim body through the opening she'd created. Once she was in, she pulled down the sliding door until it was nearly closed, leaving only a thin slit for light and air, and to avoid locking herself in.

She stood silently, waiting for her eyes to adjust. The air inside the truck box felt heavier than outside, thicker and hotter. It wasn't just a day's trapped sun. This air felt boggy, as if transported from even further South.

And the smell had gotten stronger. It went straight up her nose and into her head, giving Suzanne a light buzz. Every time she focused on it, arousal twitched through her. Her nerves, still jagged from her ministrations with the vibrator, protested, then melted into exhausted reception, the way they'd been before Thomas interrupted her.

A tendril of anxiety curled through her belly. Could this truck be transporting some sort of drug? Suzanne's rational mind didn't think so. She had never heard of a drug that turned women on by its mere proximity. Surely her heightened state was simply biological, not chemical. She had spent the entire night (up until the fight with Thomas) masturbating, and she had just been fantasizing about what the wolf-faced man would do to her if he caught her in the back of the truck. During the whole walk over here she kept thinking that the ground and the air around her smelled like pussy. She alone had spent most of the past hours priming her clit to tingle with need. So if she was still horny—so much so that she wanted to continue the night's occupation right here in the truck box—Suzanne couldn't really blame anything outside herself.

She saw only boxes in the truck's dim interior—

nothing that would obviously explain the animal smell she detected. Gingerly, Suzanne picked her way through the cramped collection. She knew from experience that a lot of truck boxes had built-in shelving on the cab end, sometimes big enough to support a small woman's weight.

She teetered a few times, but made it to the back without upsetting any of the stacked crates and packages. By now, the images in her mind drove her. If Thomas didn't like her touching herself at home in their bed, imagine what the bastard would think if he knew she planned to get herself off in the back of a stranger's truck with her panties nowhere in sight. Suzanne grinned. This was revenge without the moral concerns, and adventure with nothing to fear.

Sweat beaded on her skin in the close air, making her even more certain that everything she smelled came from herself. She found the shelves she'd been looking for, as wide and high as she hoped. They looked empty.

Suzanne reached up to check and came away with nothing more than a dusting of wood shavings on her palm. Grabbing the edge of the shelf, she tugged to check that it could support her weight. When it didn't budge, she pushed herself off a lower shelf and swung herself up.

It was even hotter on top of the shelf, with the ceiling only a couple feet away. In the small space, Suzanne didn't even have room to sit up, but she liked the sense of confinement. She took a deep breath and employed all her senses.

She could hear insects creaking and chittering

outside the truck. If the driver returned, she'd certainly hear his footsteps, and she ought to have plenty of time to slip out the way she'd come in while he got the vehicle started and warmed up.

Suzanne relaxed and stretched her body out along the shelf. The wooden surface poked her in a few places, and sawdust clung to her sweat-dampened skin wherever she touched it. She took a moment to soak in the ruggedness of her surroundings, then allowed her fingers to meander under her dress, finding her clit again.

When she spread her labia apart, her fluids escaped her pussy in viscous folds the consistency of honey. She caught some, then pulled her hand away, making the syrup stretch between cunt and fingertips in long, clear strands of arousal. Lazily, Suzanne brought her finger up to her nostrils. She liked the way she smelled.

She smelled different at different times. Tonight was her favorite, a fragrant, flowery scent that made her want to lick her finger. She did, sighing at her own salty sweetness. She'd tried eating pussy a couple times, but it had never tasted like this. If it had, Suzanne would have drank from it.

Suzanne rolled her fingertip back and forth across her tongue, dipping into her pussy a few times to refresh the flavor. She spread out her limbs as luxuriously as the shelf allowed, and only when she reached her free hand high above her head did she notice the shelf wasn't completely empty.

Her fingers nudged a wooden box, carved with some sort of intricate grooved pattern. Suzanne hadn't yet warmed up to the point of single-minded pursuit of orgasm, so she paused to see what she'd found.

She slid into a tight ball on the shelf and pulled the box into her lap. It had been made of a lovely dark wood, so polished it almost glowed in the shadows. In the poor light, she couldn't make out what its pattern represented, but the ridges and dips of it felt good against her fingertips.

A shiny metal latch held it closed, and Suzanne could not resist flipping it open. Its hinges squeaked as they revealed, lying on a bed of velvet, a long, thick dildo carved in the same style as the outside of the box, adorned with patterns Suzanne's light-starved eyes could not trace.

"Holy shit," she breathed when she saw it, then glanced around quickly. It was hard to escape the feeling she was no longer alone, hard not to perceive the dildo as a gift from a friendly observer, as impossible as that was. Was she not the only person to have masturbated on a shelf in this truck box? According to Thomas, Suzanne's desires were far from normal. Even though she didn't quite agree with him, she still had trouble imagining another woman doing exactly as she was now.

But when had other women mattered to her? Suzanne had never been the type to wonder who else had sucked a cock at the moment it passed her lips. She did not worry whether a man had bestowed similar pet names on another lover. Suzanne cared about the moment, and the moment at hand included the most incredible dildo she'd ever seen. She didn't want to waste time worrying about its owner or its past. If she'd liked how those carvings felt on her fingertips, she'd surely like them even more when they spread her pussy open.

Already, she had the dildo out of the box, rubbing it against her cheek. Its hard, smooth ridges and whorls pleased her soft skin. On impulse, her own taste still on her tongue, she flicked her tongue out and licked the carved wood.

Where she expected to taste nothing, instead Suzanne encountered a complex and compelling tang that seemed strangely familiar. Before she could think, she popped the dildo into her mouth as far as it would go. As her cheeks bulged and her tongue worried the textured wooden surface, the answer came to her. The dildo's flavor matched the smell inside the truck box.

Suzanne moaned aloud at the realization. Not allowing herself to question her actions, she yanked the dildo from her mouth and found space for it between her legs. With her pussy so wet, the thick wood slid easily into her. Her slippery fingers scrambled to control it, but her cunt had other ideas.

Almost as soon as she pressed the dildo to her entrance, her inner muscles had begun to ripple, sucking the carved wood into her. Its ridges and valleys felt like ecstasy as they passed over the mouth of her cunt, stretching it here and releasing it there.

Suzanne changed her mind about control and instead flattened her palm against the end and pushed as hard as she could. The head of the dildo butted the back of her cunt.

She writhed and bucked under the pressure she applied, raw pants spilling from her lips. With vicious abandon, she jerked it out then shoved it in again, once, twice, three times. She screamed a bit with the last stroke, suffering the sort of tortured pleasure she would have under a man bent on administering a merciless fuck.

She liked it. *Take that, Thomas*, she thought, and made herself squeal again. If her husband insisted on worrying about being replaced by a fake cock, then she'd replace him. She'd give herself the fuck of her life with this piece of wood and never look back.

Between gasps and straining muscles, she heard a footstep crunch in gravel.

Suzanne froze, holding her breath. A bead of sweat took a leisurely journey down the side of her face. Another one crested the curve of her breast.

More footsteps, headed in her direction.

"Spencer, did you hear something coming from the truck?" The speaker had a Florida accent, a little California surfer thrown into his Southern drawl.

"I'm afraid not," said Spencer, with the near courtliness of a Virginian.

"Don't you think you ought to check it out? They're paying you to take care of this cargo, aren't they? That's why you're eating pie on my dime?"

Suzanne's pulse sped up. She started to pull out the dildo, but quickly stopped, biting her lip. She couldn't remove it from her battered pussy without making herself cry out.

She needed Spencer to win this argument. It wouldn't do to give the other man a good reason to insist on getting his way.

Someone spat in the dirt outside the truck—probably Spencer, since his voice started immediately after. "There's weird shit back there, Irv. Really weird. I've heard noises coming out of there before."

"Like animals? You know we're not supposed to be carting live animals. I think you ought to take a look, especially if there's a chance one of 'em got loose. I don't care what time it is. I will call the boss right now if I have to. This cargo will be out in the parking lot so fast it'll make your head spin. I'm not smuggling animals."

"Jesus," Spencer said. "Hold your horses. You're writing a book over there, going off on this whole thing about animals. There's no animals back there. I checked last time, remember? Back in Statesboro?"

Irv barked out a short laugh. "What is it, then?"

"The noises? I don't know. I spent hours looking, though. It smells weird, and there's some really kinky shit back there, but no animals, I swear. A couple plants, but that's it."

"Plants?" The box's corrugated metal siding clunked then rattled, as if a heavy weight had dropped against it. Suzanne imagined a bulky Irv leaning against the outside of the truck. "What the hell does a sex museum want with plants?"

"Fuck if I know, Irv. They just pay me to carry their shit around. You'll excuse me if I didn't want to get too inquisitive."

"Well, why not? They've got to have some good pictures back there. Make it a lot nicer when we stop over."

Spencer made a derisive noise. "They don't have pictures. They have ... *things*. Things your girlfriend would slap you for even knowing about. Things I wouldn't stick my dick in if my life depended on it. And plants. I don't even want to think about what you're supposed to do with those. So you'll excuse me if I'm not too eager to spend a lot more time back there with all that creepy shit."

Irv let out a loud sigh. It sounded like he clapped Spencer on the shoulder. "Fine, buddy. You've convinced me. I hope you're happy. But if we get eaten by an escaped exotic animal the next time we stop for gas, I'm blaming you. Lock it up and let's go."

Suzanne sat up suddenly, banging her head on the metal ceiling of the truck box. She shoved her fist into her mouth to stop her yelp of pain. The dildo shifted inside her, and she had to suppress a moan, too. She ignored all that, three words pulsing in her brain. *Lock it up*. Shit.

"Spencer, I know you heard whatever I just heard," Irv said from outside. "Are you sure you don't want to check it out?"

Here was Suzanne's last chance. She could call to them and confess. They could react in various ways to her half-naked presence in the back of their truck—she shivered at that. Or she could stay put and risk taking a trip to wherever they were going, apparently a sex museum in an undetermined distant location.

She opened her mouth but couldn't summon the guts to actually make any noise. Footsteps came closer. She was running out of time, but she worried that if they got wise to her presence, they'd kick her out and make her go home. Honestly, she'd rather they make her fuck them both than send her back to Thomas.

Spencer grunted and yanked the sliding door closed. Suzanne watched her window of light dwindle rapidly, then disappear. Outside the truck, she heard chains and a decisive metal *snick*. The only remaining light seeped in through a few spots on the side of the truck box, where its corrugated metal sides had been stapled together imperfectly.

If she didn't jump up now and pound on that sliding door, she'd be along for the ride, locked into the super-heated metal box of the truck with no food or water as far as she knew. This couldn't be about pride anymore. Keeping quiet meant prolonged discomfort or worse.

Suzanne shoved her forearm in her mouth and yanked out the dildo, biting down through her scream of pain and pleasure. Then she moved through the cargo as fast as she could. She still hesitated to catch their attention, but she knew she had no choice. She lifted her hand and smacked the flat of her palm against the inside of the sliding door. Once. Twice. She waited, but nothing happened.

A moment later, the truck engine roared to life, explaining the lack of response from her inadvertent captors. Irv and Spencer had moved away before she'd gotten herself together, and now they couldn't hear her.

The reality of Suzanne's situation crashed down on her, creating a tumbling sensation in the pit of her stomach. Wild fantasies had been fine as long as she only played with acting on them. By allowing herself to be locked inside the truck box, Suzanne had gone way too far.

She rushed back across the box, to the cab side. There, she banged in earnest, shouting. Gears shifted, and the truck moved backward, then forward, then began to accelerate steadily. Suzanne pressed her ear to the side of the box and heard nothing but motion and vibration. If Irv and Spencer still conversed, she couldn't tell. She concluded they couldn't hear her either.

She'd left herself with no choice but to ride this out until they stopped again. For the next several hours at least, she was imprisoned with a collection of curiosities bound for a sex museum.

Her pussy pulsed as she recalled what Spencer had said about the contents of the boxes all around her. Other than dildos, what sort of things could he have been talking about? Suzanne bit her lip and grinned. "I've got nothing else to do," she said out loud, and reached for the nearest container.

She struggled to pull the wooden box into her lap. It weighed more than its size would suggest. Suzanne pried it open from one corner and poked at its contents. Bits of wood and bone lay in velvet grooves. In the dark interior of the truck box, Suzanne couldn't see them well enough to guess at their purposes. She explored with her fingers, encountering smooth, cool surfaces embellished with intricate ridges.

Were these objects meant to be used on women or men? Did they wrap around a nipple or slide into an asshole? Would they capture a cock or rub against a pussy's inner walls? She couldn't be sure, but as she touched them, the images they evoked made her tremble with even greater arousal.

She lifted out the box's first layer and found another bed of velvet. This time, her fingertips encountered hooks, rings, and barbs. She picked up a piece of bone and held it close to her face, squinting at it in the dim light. Its scooped, clawed shape suggested it was made to attach and cling, and probably to hurt. Suzanne turned it slowly. She could imagine it fitted over a man's balls, or possibly over a breast.

Once again, temptation followed thought with lightning speed. She shifted her weight in order to slip her dress out from under her and ruck it up under her armpits. Her bared breasts quivered slightly as the truck rolled steadily over the highway. Suzanne touched the bone to her nipple, tensing with anticipation even though the antique white object did little more than poke her.

She pushed against it, forcing it onto her breast. Now she winced with real discomfort. Its edges turned out to be sharper than they looked, and something about its design made it slide forward much more easily than it could be pulled back.

Suzanne tugged the bone object gingerly, hoping to

ease it off her breast. Its claws dug into her soft flesh and would not let go. She took a deep breath and attempted patience. Bracing the carved device with one hand, she squeezed and manipulated her breast in an attempt to ease it out of the bone prison where she had entrapped it.

No matter what Suzanne did, the object settled ever more firmly, trapping her nipple and gripping her breast more tightly. Its points created harsh indents, interrupting the smooth curve of her skin. Within the ring of its grasp, blood filled her breast and made her nipple swell, creating exquisite sensitivity that made her wish for a mouth to suck her there.

Her heart began to pound again as she imagined herself facing the men driving the truck with this *thing* attached to her tit. It would announce, more certainly even than the scent of her cunt, exactly what she'd been doing during her hours of confinement.

She pulled harder, but snatched her hand away with a cry when the device scraped her cruelly enough to leave a ridge of raised, irritated skin in its wake. Suzanne stared down at it, fear and lust battling inside her. She should never have experimented so boldly with these strange devices. On the other hand, her distended nipple now pulsed in time with her heartbeat, and the sensation was undeniably exciting.

She thought of the orgasms she'd lost that night— one interrupted by Thomas and another by the return of the truckers. She could retrieve that wooden dildo and slide it back into her well-slicked pussy. A few flicks to the thing attached to her breast would take her straight back to the brink of twitching desperation, she was sure. If she had to be trapped this thoroughly, why not give herself at least this much?

Suzanne shivered at the thought. How many nights had she spent trying to satisfy herself while Thomas worked? On those occasions, no matter how many times she came or how long she strained for pleasure, she never quite found what she needed. She could never fully abandon herself to her pursuit, whether it was due to worry about lost sleep or the ever-shortening hours until Thomas's return or simply the fear of blowing out her vibrator's motor. Stuck in Summerton, afraid to take someone up on the offer to get her out of there. Stuck in her marriage, afraid to really make demands. She'd even been stuck in masturbation, afraid to give herself up to it for fear she'd never be able to stop.

Now, she was leaving Summerton whether she liked it or not, and Thomas wasn't the type to take her back if she couldn't account for where she'd been. Suzanne began to sense a glimmer of freedom, the dangerous thrill of knowing she'd stepped far outside the bounds of normal life.

She wanted to find out how far her body wanted to take her. She wanted to know what else the objects in this truck could offer her.

She removed another tray from the box she'd been exploring and rifled through the new set of objects she'd revealed. Even without being able to see, she couldn't mistake the flared bases she discovered at the ends of squat, swollen twists of wood.

Suzanne caught her breath. She'd seen butt plugs online, but never used one. At any other time, she would have been afraid, but with the bone clasp biting into her breast, the odd, heady smell of the truck box, and hours of arousal behind her, curiosity and lust seemed to be the only sensations with the power to move her.

She closed her hand around one of the pieces, its polished wood surface warming to her touch. Given that her pussy still wept with frustrated desire, she didn't lack for lubrication. Suzanne scooped her arousal onto the carved plug, tracing its grooves with her thumbnail as she did. When she'd made it slippery, she stood, a little awkwardly, and braced one foot on top of a nearby box.

She felt the texture of the road running by beneath the truck's wheels, transferred through the bottom of the box, but her footing remained stable enough. She held onto a crate with one hand while reaching behind her with the other. The tip of the carved plug slipped easily between her ass cheeks and settled against the little pucker at their center.

Suzanne leaned forward, hissing when she brushed her bone-covered breast against the edge of a box. She gathered her courage, reasoning this couldn't be any more uncomfortable than the handful of times she'd allowed Thomas to fuck her in the ass. This plug was smaller than his cock, and she actually wanted it. Furthermore, it was so well lubricated and wet from her pussy that she could barely hold onto it. She took a deep breath, relaxed, and pushed.

As with every object she'd found in the truck so far, the plug slipped inside her with almost frightening ease. Her ass welcomed it to a degree she could never have expected, opening around the tip as she pressed it in bit by bit. It entered her ass with sharp pleasure, but no pain. Suzanne panted, more sweat dripping from her body to the boxes and floor beneath her. She let her weight drop onto the nearest box, and the resulting spike of sensation around her imprisoned nipple only made her press against it more. She rested briefly, but once she started, she knew she wouldn't stop until she got the entire plug inside her.

Her face screwed up with exertion, she pushed until the flared base of the thing settled between her ass cheeks. It made her pussy feel tight and achy to be so empty when her ass was so full. Suzanne imagined waddling to retrieve her wooden dildo, but she wanted to save that moment for some sort of finale.

She resisted the urge to make herself come, and instead reached for another box.

This box was considerably bigger, and as soon as she cracked the lid on this one, that damp, sexual smell rolled out in a thick cloud. She almost slammed the box closed in alarm, but again she couldn't resist plumbing its secrets.

Her clit twitched in response to the earthy scent of the box's contents. Suzanne set the lid to the side and peered inside. The faint light just allowed her to make out leaves and petals.

Plants, Spencer had said. Apparently, he'd been

right. Other than that this thing smelled like a dozen aroused cunts, Suzanne couldn't imagine what a sex museum would want with it either.

She leaned closer, holding her breath without really knowing why. The plant inside the box seemed to lie in wait, its purples and oranges expanding and contracting as if to the rhythm of an unseen pulse.

Its leaves furled around a thick, hairy stem, covered with a pale, spiny fuzz that reminded Suzanne of nothing more than pubes growing back after having been shaved bare. Its single flower dominated the center of the box, gourd-shaped and obscene. Whiskers undulated around the fleshy lips of the flower, and it glistened with beads of moisture that came from no apparent source. Suzanne shifted her angle to get a better look and wound up with her face directly above the flower. From there, she could not doubt that the flower, perhaps along with others like it, was responsible for the sexual aroma that filled the truck box. Inside the gourd, she saw a pool of viscous-looking liquid that seemed very much like the copious juices that still spilled from her own cunt. It glowed with slight phosphorescence.

She reached a hand toward the flower, then drew back, hesitating. Even if she'd been willing to stick strange objects up her ass and into her cunt, and to get her nipple stuck inside a sadistic primitive device, Suzanne worried what this thing might do to her if she touched it. She thought of poison. She thought of the way that smell affected her.

Then she remembered the flavor she'd tasted on the

wooden dildo and again she just had to know. Darting her hand in and out as quickly as she could manage, she brushed a bit of the flower's dew onto her fingertip and brought it to her nose. She inhaled deeply, and could not help closing her eyes and moaning her appreciation.

This was the scent she'd dreamed about in any fantasy she'd ever had about pussy, as sweet and bold as the best vintage of her own arousal. If she ever met a woman who smelled like this, she'd be on her knees with her head under that girl's skirt before anyone realized what had happened. Suzanne's mouth fell open at the thought, her tongue reaching.

"I wouldn't do that just yet," a voice said from a corner of the truck box.

Suzanne screamed full-out, jumping clear of the crate containing the alluring flower. "Who the hell is there?"

Alarm rushed through her, but also shame. If she wasn't alone in the truck box, that meant someone had seen her play with her pussy and suck a wooden dildo. She hadn't been alone when she attached a strange object to her nipple and shoved a butt plug of indeterminate origin up her ass.

"My name is Karl Arnold," the voice said. "This collection used to belong to me." Now that her shock was wearing off, Suzanne noticed that the voice sounded muffled.

"Where are you?" She scraped her gaze over every available surface and saw no movement, nothing that rose and fell with breath. She couldn't imagine where the voice's owner could be hiding, unless … "Are you inside a *box*?"

"Incidentally, yes. Come and see."

Suzanne stared in the direction of the voice, suddenly self-conscious. She had the urge to arrange her dress for modesty, as impossible as that seemed. She shifted her weight from one foot to the other in indecision, inadvertently causing herself to sigh and moan as the butt plug moved inside her. One hand flew back to its base. She wondered if she should pull it out. Suzanne didn't know which was worse—approaching this man when he knew she had a butt plug in her ass, or removing the butt plug when she knew he might watch her do it.

Soft laughter echoed through the humid metal box. "Don't be shy, girl. You certainly weren't before."

Suzanne sighed. If she'd had any hope that he *hadn't* seen every moment of her performance, he'd just put an end to it. She took a reluctant step in the direction of the voice.

"If I've learned anything about you in the last couple hours, you're going to find this very interesting," the man coaxed. Suzanne wished she had a little more resistance, but she couldn't help it—she was dying to find out the circumstances under which this man had been able to hide for so long.

She went to the corner, opposite from the shelf where she'd discovered the dildo. Her breath fluttered unevenly as she moved. Every footfall and muscle twitch affected the butt plug and the bone claw. "Where are you?" Suzanne whispered. Her voice came out sounding strangled.

"Open the big crate you're standing next to. It opens

from the side."

With trembling hands, Suzanne loosened the metal latches that fastened the crate shut. She had to pause several times to rearrange and restack boxes in order to make space for the side of the crate to swing open. Each time she did, she wondered how well he could see her and if he was watching. By now, she felt like her dirty dress covered less than nothing.

Finally, Suzanne cleared enough space, somewhat trapping herself in the corner in the process. "Look, just don't do anything crazy, please," she said, and opened the crate.

The hinged wooden side of it banged against the wall of boxes Suzanne had created. It threatened to send a few of them toppling, but she paid no attention. Her hand flew to her mouth as she stared into the crate's interior.

This flower was much larger than the other she'd discovered—it grew as high as her shoulder. The same fuzzy leaves covered the vines that wound around it and trailed all over the inside of the box. If possible, the flower's venereal smell was even more intense than before. The truck box grew several increments brighter when she opened the crate, thanks to the weird glow that emanated from the sweet-smelling fluid dripping from the flower's petals and rimming its fleshy lips.

All those facts faded to the background, however, at the sight of the man who seemed to grow out of the flower's core. She saw a face and a head—handsome, though a little old for her—but the man's body was completely obscured and wrapped by petals and leaves. Bright blue eyes stared at her from a lined, careworn face. Hair tangled with the vines that surrounded him. Gleaming fluid dripped from the petals and ran down his face, streaking him with eerie, glowing tracks. "What the hell?" Suzanne breathed the words rather than speaking them.

The man smiled. "You're even better-looking now that I've got a clear view."

Suzanne crossed her arms over her chest, yelping when she brushed the bone clamp. She scowled and fixed Karl Arnold with the sternest stare she could manage given her compromising position. "Are you ... Is the plant ..." She trailed off and shook her head. "I don't understand."

"The plant is a symbiote, if that's what you're asking. "It feeds me and gives me shelter. I do my best to return the favor."

"Is it hurting you?"

He smiled. "The symbiosis is extremely pleasurable."

"Can you ... can you get away from it if you want to?"

"In a manner of speaking." He wriggled within the plant's apparently tight embrace. After a few moments of struggle, his shoulders emerged. The plant protested with a sucking sound as he proceeded to draw one arm out of its folds. His arm glistened from fingertip to armpit with the flower's juices. "Help me out, will you?"

Suzanne stared at him.

"I'll get out eventually either way, it'll just take longer

if you don't work with me."

She relented and took his hand. He was so slippery she had to squeeze as hard as she could to maintain her grip on him. She braced herself and pulled his arm with all her strength. Little by little, the plant was forced to relinquish him.

He emerged naked, very gaunt, and coated from head to toe. His half-hard cock lifted its head at her. Karl noticed Suzanne's scrutiny. "I'd give you a more proper salute, but it keeps me milked pretty good."

Suzanne dropped to a sitting position, the bizarre man before her making her briefly forget about the butt plug she wore. But when the plug's wooden base made contact with the edge of a crate, Suzanne was reminded anew and she stifled a cry as Karl grinned. She resisted the urge to lay into him for that. "Can you explain any of this to me?"

"In the forests of Brunei, carnivorous plants sometimes form symbiotic relationships with animals. They provide places to nest, say, and feed off the animals' discarded organic matter. This is a refinement of the principle."

Suzanne gaped at him. "Are you saying that plant was eating you?"

"Me personally? No. Feeding off my cum? Yes. The pitcher is filled with a powerful aphrodisiac. Some enthusiasts believe it's synthesized from the sexual fluids of its symbiotic partners. The specimens in the truck all come from the most prized line."

"And you were just … riding in one of them? Like a

passenger? Inside of a box locked from the outside?"

Karl looked embarrassed for a moment. He touched his cock a little self-consciously. "Everyone thinks I'm missing, I believe. Or they wouldn't have sold my collection. I don't always, uh, come up for air."

"Most of the time, not even your head comes out of that plant?"

"Indeed. The plant protects me quite securely. It can be difficult to tell that there's anyone inside."

"The plant is very … aromatic."

"And yet the plant and I could both smell you," Karl said, with a leer that made Suzanne stand up and back away a few steps. "Admit it, you're curious."

"I know this may be hard to believe considering the things you just watched me do, but I do draw the line somewhere. I think getting sexually involved with a carnivorous plant is it."

"You tasted it, didn't you?" Karl's tongue licked over his lips. "You know how good it is."

"Stay back. I'm not kidding." The backs of Suzanne's legs hit the corrugated metal siding. She had nowhere to go.

"My collection is very specialized," Karl said. "Every object comes from the same part of the world. Each piece is designed to elicit responses that will be pleasing to the plant. The plant's secretions lower inhibitions. You came in so well-lubricated, so prepared to experiment with yourself, that I couldn't help wondering whether you'd been affected by the plant's secretions at quite a distance."

"I just get very horny sometimes," Suzanne protested. She realized how ridiculous she sounded as soon as the sentence came out of her mouth. Her stomach twisted when Karl answered with a slow, lascivious grin.

"Don't you want to see how it can make you feel?" He covered the distance between them in just a few steps. His naked body pressed against hers, the plant's juices soaking through her abused dress, sticking to her bare skin. The feeling was obscenely warm.

Suzanne wasn't sure how well she could fight him. She pressed back against the side of the truck box as hard as she could and kept a wary eye on Karl.

He lifted coated fingers to her cheek, smearing the plant's pungent aroma across the skin there. He traced a line that ended at the corner of her mouth. "Taste it again," Karl whispered. "For me." He stood so close that he caused the butt plug and bone clamp to torment and please her.

Suzanne whimpered. She didn't want this to go too far, but hadn't it gone too far the moment she found the wooden dildo? Certainly by the moment she allowed herself to get locked inside the truck box. And Thomas had thought it went too far the moment he found out how tirelessly she could use a vibrator.

Screw all of that, she thought. Thomas didn't know what "too far" even meant, and until this moment Suzanne had only a hazy comprehension of the idea herself. She glared at Karl defiantly and flicked her tongue out rapidly, tasting the bead of fluid he'd left at the edge of her lip.

She did want to drink it. It was fresher than what had coated the dildo, and far more potent. She wanted to plunge her face in it and lap it up while she masturbated furiously. Of course it was all over Karl's skin, and she realized she wanted to lick every inch of him.

He smiled. "That's my girl." His hand crept to her breast, to the bone clamp.

Suzanne watched his fingers. He repulsed and fascinated her at the same time. She wondered how easily she could turn into him. Would she end up like him if she gave herself over to her desires? She meant to find out.

She buried her face in Karl's neck and breathed in that scent. She didn't really believe the flower's juices could change her actions. At best, they might provide an excuse. She sucked on his pale skin while he fiddled with the device that trapped her nipple.

It got tighter and tighter until she gasped and arched backward. "Oh my God, that hurts," she sighed.

His fingers curled into her pussy. "You like for it to hurt, don't you?"

"Especially there," Suzanne said.

"Then let me get your dildo again. I've got a surprise for you."

She waited, her breast aching and her tongue still celebrating the flavor of the plant. Karl returned a moment later and shoved the wooden dildo into Suzanne with no further preamble. She writhed in response to it, opening her legs as wide as she could to take it as far as possible.

"How long would you have fucked yourself if you hadn't been interrupted?" Karl asked.

"Until I had to stop," Suzanne said, her voice as defiant as her eyes had been earlier. "Until I needed water or food."

"And you didn't even know everything it could do." He reached between her legs and turned a knob, and the dildo *opened* inside her, dozens of rods expanding from its surface and pressing against her where she didn't really have room to accommodate more. They created a dull pain up and down the inside of her pussy, especially where they shared a wall with the butt plug.

"What is that?" Suzanne ground out the words, barely managing them.

"Don't worry. This version of the device isn't meant to cause harm. It's not coming out of your pussy until the catch is released, but it won't really hurt you." Karl gripped her around the waist and turned her around.

She began to ask another question, then pulled up short when she realized his likely target. Her ass tensed. "I—"

Before she could gather herself enough to speak, he twisted a knob in the wooden base and her ass flourished into the most excruciating pleasure. The plug fought for space with the dildo that stuffed her cunt full. Suzanne felt spread from within.

Words seemed an utter impossibility, and Karl did not allow her room for them. She turned again and he fed his flesh to her, pushing his nectar-coated skin between her lips.

Lost in wordless, ecstatic agony, Suzanne suckled whatever he offered her almost blindly. Her hips thrust at empty air. Her cunt and anus struggled to accommodate her various intruders, and were all the happier for it.

Suzanne barely noticed when Karl made her walk. He guided her back to the plant, and all she noticed was the softness of its leaves. He kissed her and she let him. He tasted like the plant, only sour.

His fingers slipped between her legs and found her clit. Suzanne jerked and pulled back. "I can't come when I'm stretched open like this. I'll come too hard, and it'll hurt."

"Shhh," Karl said. "You want to come, don't you? You've been after that big orgasm for so long." He spoke with total sympathy, as if he had indeed known her innermost thoughts these past years.

Suzanne spread her legs for him. He praised her, then set about strumming and rolling her clit until she would have fallen straight into the plant if she hadn't been so afraid of it. Her body tightened.

Just before she came, she made one more panicked noise of protest.

"No," Karl told her. "Good girl. That's it."

Orgasm ripped through her. The expanded dildo and butt plug didn't give her spasms anywhere to go. She was forced to rely on Karl to hold her on her feet. She felt herself dripping, drooling, spurting, and she imagined that fleshy plant soaking her up. She screamed and wailed and struggled, but it felt like his devices were milking her, turning her inside out. That damn orgasm never wanted to end.

Still in the throes of it, she only dimly noticed the truck slowing, then tilting slightly to one side as it pulled off the highway and onto the tight circle of an exit ramp. Only when the driver hit the brakes and she fell against Karl did she fully realize that they'd stopped traveling, and that her first opportunity to escape might have come.

"Let me out, Karl," Suzanne said, already fumbling between her legs in case he did not comply. "These things have me stretched too far."

"It seemed like they had you stretched just far enough," Karl observed, but he brushed her fingers out of the way and deftly located the hidden catches that relieved the pressure inside her. Her cunt clenched at the change, and the wooden dildo shot out of her, hitting the floor of the truck with a clang. He did something to the object biting into her breast, and it too fell away.

"Spencer, you *cannot* keep claiming there's nothing wrong back there," Irv's voice said from just outside. "What the hell was that clank? What the hell was that goddamn *scream* I heard a few minutes back. And the one just now. If you don't check it out, I'm going to do it myself."

Karl sighed. "Sorry, sweetheart. I don't want to deal with this. I'm, uh, more comfortable in there anyway." Before Suzanne could protest, he pressed one foot into the plant's fleshy opening, then the other. She watched open-mouthed as it accepted him, sucking his entire body in with a smooth, muscular motion. Even his head disappeared this time, transforming him into an oddly shaped bulge attached to the side of a very strange-looking plant. Karl didn't seem likely to surface again anytime soon.

A moment later a sharp click and metal rapping on metal announced the opening of the outer lock. If Suzanne hadn't been in such an odd position, she might have raced for the opening as soon as Spencer slid the door up, hoping to bowl past him and gain her freedom by the element of surprise. As it was, her massive orgasm had left her knees so weak that she wouldn't be running anywhere for at least a quarter of an hour.

Suzanne had no choice but to stand where she was, blinking in the light. Her eyes hadn't adjusted yet, so she couldn't see the expressions on Irv and Spencer's faces. She did, however, hear their simultaneous gasps at the sight of her.

"Jesus Henry Christ on crutches," Irv breathed. Suzanne thought about how she must look, arousal dribbling down her legs, her nipple swollen from the bone clamp and a dress that probably didn't do much of anything anymore.

Staring out the back of that hot little truck box, she suddenly knew how to get out of town on her own terms. There had to be a lot of plants back here, enough to welcome two new symbiotes and leave the truckers pleasurably impeded for Suzanne to take their keys and wallets.

The two men swung themselves into the back of truck box. Suzanne indeed recognized the wolf-faced man from the diner. He gave her that same hungry look, like he'd had a fat dick for days and all he wanted to do was fuck her. She was going to enjoy this. She was going to take her time.

After this, she wouldn't ever have to go back to Thomas, and she wouldn't ever have to hold herself back from anything.

Suzanne reached back with one hand and scooped a gooey handful of fluid from the plant behind her. With the other hand, she reached between her legs. "Do you boys want to try a taste test?"

She knew they wouldn't resist.

PACKING STEEL

LANA FOX

Packing Steel

—◇◇◇—

Chapter 1

From the moment I'd seen Michaela's photo, I'd been on fire for her. Yeah, that's right—a jaded hitter like me, who'd been killing professionally for seven years. I, who couldn't climax any more, let alone have a crush, was obsessed with a girl in a polka-dot dress. And when I say "obsessed," make no mistake, *elle m'enflammait*—we're talking serious fire.

My boss, Odette, had first shown me that photo when she'd called me in to her underground office, two weeks before. When I turned up, it was raining hard, making the streets of Paris flood. That made me feel better about the slate walls, the low lighting, and wall-hung pictures of filmstars with guns. Odette had a thing about being armed and had once advised me, woman-to-woman, *de femme à femme*, to always pack steel. In fact, it was this love of guns that had launched her into the business. According to Odette, her *Papa* hadn't wanted her to walk in his footsteps. But every time she'd seen a gun, her face had lit up, and by the time she reached eighteen, he relented and trained her himself.

Odette had become notorious.

Then again, so had I.

She offered me a whisky, which I refused; and a cigarette, which I took. As I lit up, I thought about screwing her. Not that I thought my clit could get hard any more, but hell, a woman can dream. So what if Odette killed her own people and was twenty years older than me? With the gentle lines on her unpowdered face, and the soft lips and fierce green eyes, not to mention those curves beneath her pleather dress, Odette must have been one hell of a lay.

She invited me to sit in the typist's chair near her desk—the chair reserved for guests. I swiveled the seat, so the back was facing her, before sitting astride it in my leather trousers, with my arms draped over the seat-back, smoking in her direction. She laughed dryly, lit her own cigarette. You had to play it cool with Odette, and sitting in that cheap little chair made you feel lower than she was. But I'd found ways to fuck with that. What you don't fear can't hurt you.

In fact, just a week before that, I'd stood in this office and told Odette that I wanted out. I'd half-expected her to shoot me on the spot, which didn't bother me, frankly. So I was surprised when she'd told me she'd been expecting me to quit. My heart wasn't in the job any more, she'd said. "But your last contract will earn your freedom. Do it well, and I'll let you go—if that's what you want. Screw up and I'll put a hole in your head. A nice, tight little hole."

Bien sûr, Odette would be a hot little screw. The sort that would send you flying. The sort that would end in an unmarked grave.

So here I was, seven days later, for the promised details of this final gig. Behind her desk, in the low glow of the angle-poise lamp, Odette leaned back in her swivel chair. "You look gloomy, *ma chère*," she said, exhaling a plume of smoke, but I didn't trust her niceties. Odette was a woman who could call you "dear" then slit your throat, *pas de problème.*

"So," I said. "The job."

She raised an eyebrow and slid a photo across the desk, before falling back into her seat, red lips glistening in the half-light. "Pretty little thing, she is. Husband wants her head."

And because irony's my fuck-buddy, I said, "What a gent."

Then everything changed, because even when my fingers first touched that photo, hitting the tacky surface as I pulled it into view—even as I smelled Odette's perfume beneath the tinge of tobacco—I knew something big was happening. I could feel it in my pulse, in the lightness of my head. I felt it in my groin, where I usually felt so little.

And then, I saw her. My final kill. She wore a red and white polka-dot dress that fell into a low V around her gorgeous cleavage, and a sash-like belt at her middle gathered in the material and gripped her full waist. She was turning to the camera, surprised *peut-être*, no smile on her face, just the beginnings of a startle. Her eyes were wide and brown, her mouth was gloriously wide, her lips plump and biteable. Brown curls fell loosely down her back, her skin as translucent as crystallized candy just begging to be licked. She had the look of a 'fifties beauty. I imagined her arranged on a pile of summer hay, her nipples hard and pink, her breasts full and luxurious, her pussy trimmed and ready, her slim fingers stroking over her belly, her hips. Her eyes—I knew already—would be innocent but tempting. I'd fuck her with a strap-on, or maybe with my fingers—Christ, I'd fuck her in every way possible. I'd moan like an animal, and she'd cry out. She wouldn't stop coming. Not ever. *Jamais.*

I was so turned on just looking at her, that my body felt different. My nipples were hard beneath my tank-top, I could even feel the tattooed skin on my arm—the black snake coiling around my bicep—prickling as if the needle were still on it. Everything felt immediate and present, as if someone had lifted a veil from my body. This woman made me want to be right inside her, all the way in, fucking her with addiction. I'd come—I was sure of it—just to push my fingers into her. I'd come, just to feel her pussy clench me, to be tight inside with my hand on one of her breasts. *Mon Dieu*, I was wet. And it felt good. Why the fuck had I forgotten this burn, this need for flesh on flesh? This long-lost longing for perfumed skin?

Seven years and I'd felt nothing. Seven years of killing and no heat.

Until now.

When I looked up at Odette, I could hear her talking

in that smoky voice. She was saying something about my British passport and the fact that the client had paid in full. But all I could focus on were Odette's breasts, pressed up inside that pleather dress. I could just see the outline of her nipples, and I could imagine how hot it would be to take her, thrusting her against the wall so that the filmstar pictures clattered to the floor, pawing her breasts, my groin against her thigh, biting those red lips until she groaned with pleasure.

Suddenly, I was desperate for a screw. And all because of an English bitch whose husband had paid in full to have me kill her. But apart from it being the key to my freedom, I hadn't yet guessed at the importance of this kill. Sure, it was a man murdering a wife. But the man wasn't just anyone.

He was Algernon Cross, the romance novelist. England's rising star. The graphic sex in his novels had earned him death threats, yet he faced them with unphased suavity. Algernon filled the gossip columns, with his gentlemanly looks and wealthy lifestyle.

When he fed the tabloid press his cock, they swallowed.

When I was younger, I could dance all night. I loved to feel the music beating up through the nightclub's floor, right into my body, right into my cunt. That's when you know you're alive, when you feel your organs vibrating, when your ribs shake, and your pussy strums, and your heart rocks around.

Well, that's how I felt after I'd seen that photo. I was full of this Michaela, and she was thumping through me, pounding into my pussy, making it hot and wet. In fact, I was so full of this woman, with her plump breasts and glowing skin, that I bought a new outfit for my Eurostar journey. *C'est vrai*, I turned up on that train in a pleated denim mini-skirt that ended half-way up my thighs and a tight wine-red top that pulled my tits in tight. Under there, I wore just the thinnest satin bra that rubbed at my nipples whenever I moved, and briefs to match. As I moved, I felt every texture, every movement, every stroke. Even the high-heeled boots, which I'd once worn to threaten a restaurant owner who'd tried to trick Odette, clutched at me differently. Michaela was making me *feel* them. Everything clutched at me with the desperation of 100 anonymous hands at a strip-club.

Turned out, I craved every person that was traveling on that train—every pussy, every cock, ever breast and thigh. Women walked past my compartment and I watched them through the glass doors, thinking of Michaela, examining the curve of their velvet-clad buttocks or the tight grip of their skinny jeans. I fantasized about fucking Michaela just before I killed her, holding a blade at her delicate throat, my other hand on her breast. She'd be naked—warm and smooth in my arms, her mouth mine to fill, her pussy mine to plunder. And she'd want me so badly, with my ready mouth, that I'd let the knife fall and I'd fuck her instead.

Baise moi, Michaela. Vitement.

But I was on assignment and she was my mark—the

last ever mark, the one to end the bloodshed—and I had to play it cool, or as Odette always said, show some "hitter steel." So I'd made sure Michaela's photo was packed away tight, and I told myself I could fuck who I liked, as long as it wasn't her.

Not far into the journey, just as the train had entered the tunnel, I was joined by a guy in a V-neck sweater, who was blond as a cherub and smelled like a men's magazine. I was all too keen to stamp out my fantasies and have him touch my body—and when you hit marks for a living, you tend to grab what you want. So I watched as he lounged in the seat to my left and glared at my thighs like a tomcat, a greedy smile on his thin lips. I grasped his hand and thrust it beneath my skirt. "If you want it," I murmured against his ear, "let's quit the niceties."

He let out a breathy moan and his eyes flared a little. He swore in an East London accent, running his hand up my thigh. "Hot for it are you, you little slut?" He stroked me slowly, and it felt good, but no one calls me *slut* then gets to drive the Merc. So I tore his flies open and pulled out his cock, making him moan so loudly that everyone must have heard. His cock wasn't large, but I don't care for large. And the hottest thing was the way it was hardening in my hand. "God, girl," he encouraged, grasping the base of his seat, his face contorting with ecstasy.

"See who's in control, *little slut*?" I said. "*Tu vois, ma petite putain?*"

He grinned like a man who likes that he's been

caught, then groaned again when I started to jerk him off a little, a small track of drool seeping down his chin as his mouth fell open wider. But I was desperate for contact myself, so I grabbed his fingers, parted my thighs and plunged his hand beneath my skirt and onto my silky briefs. It was my turn to moan, though I tried to stifle it. Can't show a bitch you're out of control. But it felt so good and he rubbed so right, harder and harder, til I was arching back, knees raised, growling for more.

After seven lonely years, my need for touch, for contact, roared back to life. I pulled down my top and pushed my tits right out of their bra. He made quick work of both breasts, flicking his tongue over them, making me grit my teeth and grind my nipple against his lips. My cunt was so wet that when he pulled away, I half-expected to look down and see a stain on my panties, as if I'd peed myself. He was jerking himself off, his cheeks and nose red with arousal, and when I tugged his hand towards my pussy and pulled aside the flimsy strip of my briefs, he pushed two fingers into me and started to fuck me hard. I'd forgotten this feeling, and it felt fucking great. So I made noise. And he did too, especially when he took back his hand to wrap it around his own cock, yanking it four or five times, before struggling up, so he was half-standing, and coming all over my tits. As he spurted, he announced (like it needed a soundtrack), "All over your tits … I'm coming … all over your … fuck …" When he pulled back, I saw myself—streaked breasts and all—reflected in the windowpane. The blackness of the tunnel made the reflection clear, and I imagined Michaela licking the glaze from my tits, her tongue flicking over me like a kitten's, her eyes all big with lust. I came in just moments, rubbing my clit, my hips bucking with the crazy-good heat, the climax bursting up through me like a geyser—the end of a seven-year drought.

Think of all the tail I'd have had over the years, if I'd seen Michaela back then and my libido had stayed awake. As I mopped the cum off my tits, I realized it wasn't just Micheala that was lighting my fire. It was the thought of escaping all the frightened faces pleading for their lives; the thought of not having to wash blood from my hair or run through the night with the sirens still wailing and my Glock still hot at my side, the memories of its shots ringing in my ears. The screams. The last breaths that I always rolled my eyes at—still do, in my way, just to keep the past hemmed in. It was enough to keep you up at night, until you learned numbness. And maybe that numbness had murdered my sex drive.

Just one more kill. Just one, then it's over.
I told myself this. Like I believed it.

Once I'd tidied myself up and watched Mr. "All-Over-Your Tits" sneak away like a shame-faced dog, a woman peered through the glass door, but I didn't get the feeling she was a mole. All the same, she might be. I mean, the mole was around here somewhere. They *had* to be. There was always a dark horse trained to track your every move, making sure you scored the hit. Yes, he—or she—would insist on seeing

Michaela's pretty head with a bullet through the temple. If I failed, just one text from this dark horse would tell Odette I was dirty goods. Then? Two options. Come clean and risk death. Or just do the death bit. And hell, I had a reason to live for now.

Still, I'd work out who the mole was, even if it wasn't her. I'd track them down, *bien sûr*.

I took a long look at the woman on the other side of the glass, before she smiled at me and turned away. She was gorgeous, wearing a red polka-dot dress. It wasn't like Michaela's dress—the one from the photo—which was flared. No, this dress was pencil-straight. But even so, the woman's outfit brought me back to that photo, and made me think of raising Michaela's skirt, pulling down her briefs and spanking the crap out of her. Oh I'd make her whinnie! I'd make her beg for more. And those innocent eyes—that sweet, innocent stare—would be filled with sin, *plein à craquer*.

So I followed the woman in the red polka-dots, telling myself she might indeed be a mole—though really I knew she wasn't. And it only took a couple of lines, followed by a game of wit, for me to get her into the tiny WC. Then, there I was, spanking her tanned ass cheeks, getting her to call me Miss as she quivered and convulsed. "Oh do it again, *Maman*! *Si, si*!" and I spanked her red and sore until she wailed out her climax.

After, all red-faced and cute, I got her to unbutton her dress. God, she was young and exquisite—twenty-one, if that. Her scent was a mixture of Chanel and liquorice.

Her hair was auburn, falling down her back. And when she'd unbuttoned the front of that dress, I dipped inside and felt her soft little breasts, peaked with a pair of small, hard nipples. My cunt was hot and wet. I knew what I wanted. So I got the girl down on her knees, while I leaned back against the wall, her head half-hidden beneath my pleated skirt, and she licked my clit until I was on the brink. Then, out of control, I grasped her head, pulling her mouth onto me hard, as I ground down to meet her pressure, milking every last bit from that fiery climax. Sweet girl, she worked the come from me almost as well as Michaela would.

Dieu, it was hot.

It was like dying to music.

Cards-on-the-table time. Here's why the thought of ending up in London didn't exactly fill me with joy.

I'd been born in the Big Smoke, as my father used to call it, thirty years earlier, to a French mother and a British dad. (Dual passport. Bilingual. Beyond that, the high points are hard to spot.) My parents ditched me at sixteen when they caught me on my bed with my friend Chao Mai, one hand inside her little black skirt. (That girl had the tightest butt I've ever groped.) My family, if you can call them that, were racists and homophobes, who didn't realize they'd raised a natural criminal, and a girl who'd screw anything that moved. It's strange they were surprised, especially since they'd been waiting for me to 'fuck up' for over a decade.

What can I say? I don't disappoint.

After my family threw me out, leaving me homeless, I used my French passport and a wad of stolen money to catch a boat to France then hitchhike to Nantes where I could stay with my cousin, Philippe. Philippe was two years my senior, and was studying medicine or something like that at the *Université de Nantes*. The important thing was, he had an apartment of his own, and we'd always gotten along. I slept on his floor and screwed my way through a year or two— sometimes fucking for fun, sometimes fucking for money. Then, thanks to one of my regular johns, I got myself a job at a fast food restaurant that served mussels with fries—*moules frites*.

Merde, I was a useless waitress. I've never even liked shellfish.

I soon worked out that pick-pocketing made easier money than working on my back. And what also made it a win was the thought of my parents' faces if they ever learned how I made my way. Dipping in pockets, while flirting with a mark. Ripping the tags off expensive clothes. And months later, breaking into offices and stealing papers for bastards— now that got me the kind of cash that meant I could pay my own rent. I became well-known. Got hired by people you can't piss off.

Then Odette found me at age nineteen and told me I had talent. No one had ever said that before. "I'm offering you crime," she said. "When has crime ever let you down?"

I said, "Not ever."

I liked her.

Chapter 2

Modern-day London was a strange mix. From the top deck of a double-decker bus, I watched giant silvery buildings that looked like glassy bullets, fog-laden bridges, and vast gray churches with dozens of spires. I recognized the old bits, but not the new. Even the sky wasn't like it used to be—the clouds hung lower now, like mold on fruit.

Thankfully, this wasn't the old suburb where I'd grown up—it was the throbbing center, all tourists and cathedrals, taxis and protests, piercings and suits. Here, punks and merchant bankers walked past one another, hardly noticing each other. They were free, those people. At least, they seemed free to me. No hits, no crimes, no being shot if they didn't deliver.

But fuck, you never know what people's lives are like.

Alors, on the bus, I could feel that mole I mentioned earlier, watching my every move. Was it the businessman sitting behind me, with black hair and a neat side-parting? Was it the woman to my left, with the pierced nose and scant covering of acne, who seemed glued to her Agatha Christie novel? Or was it the eerie boy with the sallow face and angular cheekbones, who was listening to rock music on a pair of earbuds? I'd caught all three of them watching me. But so what? The bus was packed and I was eye-fodder, thanks to my short skirt and boots.

It was nice. Being stared at was making me horny.

On every hit I scored from Odette, she tried to control where I was and when. On this trip, her people had booked me into a chain hotel near Piccadilly. It wasn't the Ritz, but it was smart compared to the dumps I was usually booked into. Either Odette wanted to treat me, or she wanted to tempt me into staying on as a hitter. With that bitch you never knew.

Did I mention that I liked her?

Of course, Odette's folks had managed this trip *parfaitment*. I arrived at reception, certain I was still being watched, and was handed a suitcase by the blonde behind the desk. "Your Uncle Stan left this for you," she told me, but as she handed it across, she didn't meet my eye. God knows what "Uncle Stan" had promised her in exchange for keeping this bag behind the desk.

Uncle Stan played "uncle" to all of Odette's hitters. He—or she—left us tidbits in cases, hidden beneath clothes, in secret compartments. Weapons, a handgun, an identity badge—that sort of thing. Uncle Stan had ways of sweet-talking receptionists. I liked to imagine him promising everyone money and sex, and had often pictured him as a woman, not a guy—a slick brunette with an ass that made you pant. As I was leaving reception, I imagined fucking this sexy Uncle Stan, riding her strapped-on cock as she sucked my fingers and moaned.

Up in my room, I explored the case for goodies. I found a small handgun, an explosive device that looked like a mobile phone, a pack of painkillers that would knock you out cold, and lastly—a thoughtful little touch—some killer pills for murders or suicides, depending on the sitch. There was also a fake ID in there to help get me into the launch party for Algernon Cross's recent release—this was where I'd agreed to kill Miss Michaela.

When I took out that gun, I imagined trailing the barrel down Michaela's pale body, watching the steel make her nipples harden, watching her tremble with fear and desire … The thought made me feel weak in my legs, horny in my groin. I'd never been one of those hitters who gets turned on by shooting a mark, but right now I was changing. The thought of killing Michaela, up close and personal, made my heart speed up and my pussy burn. In fact, I had to take a shower and rub one out just to keep myself sane.

Afterward, thanks to Uncle Stan's packing, I dressed in stilettos and a fitted black dress, and stuffed my shoulder bag with subtle little weapons. The identity badge that was pinned above my left breast said, "Juliette de Neuve, Journalist: *Marie Claire*, Paris." I mouthed the new name in the mirror as I touched up my lipstick.

Au revoir, Jae Steele. *Bonsoir*, Juliette de Neuve.

Algernon and Michaela Cross lived in Surrey. To get to their countryside home, which was more like a fucking mansion, I had to take a train, followed by a cab. I'd never seen a home so grand, standing by itself, surrounded by rolling hills, grazing sheep, and trees galore. So this was where Algernon Cross had his horses groomed, his steaks cooked rare, and, now and then, a loved one quietly killed.

To enter, I had to climb massive stone steps, flanked by vast pillars. You could tell I was late. There was no one else around, but I could feel eyes on me just the same. Somewhere the mole was hiding, waiting for me to arrive.

I entered a vast marble entrance hall. By a chair and table, a black man in a tux with an American accent, and muscles that could knock you into tomorrow, asked if he could look through my bag. *Over the Queen's dead backside*, I thought to myself.

Fucking security. It gets me every time.

The options: I could shoot pretty boy, but bodies are a burden and gunfire's a giveaway. Plus I was on fire for a screw—and hell, this guy would have a cock to ride. So I leaned towards him, pressed a hand on his heavy chest and said, "Check my bag after you've checked the rest of me, big boy."

I saw his eyes flare, then he glanced down at my tits. When he looked back up, he was husky with lust. "Oh I'll give you a thorough checking, babe. If you empty your handbag first."

Merde. I was just warming up to him.

I pretended to have left something in the car, and did a swift 180.

Et alors, you know who was less fuckable than Mr. Security? The Chief Gardener who I had to blow in order to use a back entrance. After a mouthful of gross cum—which I swear tasted like soil—he let me in through the cellar, past crates of dusty wine bottles, then up through the kitchen past giggling staff who'd probably guessed what this favor had cost me. Up the servants' stairs we went and out onto a landing. Then the lucky dog abandoned me, a spring in his step, keys jangling from the belt on his jeans.

Et bien, it had been worth it. I was inside.

Turns out, Michaela lived in an oak-paneled prison. There were fuck-off massive paintings that belonged in a museum, and a huge statue nestled in an alcove: a naked woman wrestling with a swan. The floor was like a chessboard, and the lamp above was a chandelier. The whole place smelled like the furniture wax my mother had always used to buff the fucking piano. Looking down over the banisters, I saw the polished hallway that I'd have crossed if I'd gotten through the screening.

Suddenly, applause rose from somewhere to my right. I stared down the corridor to see an open door—through it, I glimpsed people wearing dresses, hats and expensive suits. They were listening to a speaker, clapping their hands and mewing with pleasure like only the posh know how. Algernon was speaking, I guessed. He'd told Odette he'd try and keep Michaela nearby, so she was easy to find and kill. I checked I had my pass pinned to my dress, and I headed towards them.

Then suddenly I heard Michaela.

Don't ask me how I knew it was her. But I did, straight away. She was saying, "Can't you just leave me alone for a minute, boys? I'll be good, I promise." It was a weird thing to say, but I was distracted by that sexy voice: posh, with a soft little rasp, and an irony that rang through it. I turned, pulse beating, heat in my cunt.

And there she was.

She was climbing the staircase, talking to two security guards—one on either side of her. Her dark curly hair was braided like a girl's, and her skin was the kind of pale that made milk seem dark. She was bigger than she'd looked in the photo, and I liked that a lot—that curvy buxom look. In a poppy-print dress, her breasts were globed up, held tight by the fabric. Perfect breasts, bulging and smooth, the kind that get you horny again when you've only just come, and lips that looked cherry-stained. Sure, she was hot. But it was more than that.

She was my perfect fucking screw.

I reached for my gun, without even thinking—put my hand on my handbag to feel the steel inside. One of the men—a butch redhead, with a Gucci watch that blinked silver in the light—was telling Michaela she had to be "accompanied."

I didn't like his tone, so I called out, "Says who?"

All three of them turned my way. I might as well have said, *Busted!*

"Says the Boss," said Mr. Redhead. "Says the Boss of

everyone here."

"Wow," I said, with all the irony I could scrape. "Well, he must be scary then."

The boys didn't like that. They exchanged a sour glance, while Michaela gave me a sultry look that, if I wasn't on a hit, could make my pussy drip down my thighs.

One of the men—the older one with a graying crew-cut and the jowls of a bulldog—had caught hold of her wrist like she was his prisoner.

"Who are you?" Michaela asked me, without even trying to shake him off.

Fuck, she was beautiful. "Jae," I told her. Then I had to add that it was a nickname, because I was wearing this stupid journalist's badge with "Juliette" on it.

Merde.

"You're a guest?" she said, with a tiny smile. *I could kiss that lipstick off you,* I thought. When I told her I was here for the book launch, she didn't take her eyes from mine. I could feel that fascinated stare, as she walked right up to me, the men following.

She tapped my ID tag. "A journalist."

"For my sins."

"Is that a French accent?"

"*Bien sûr.* I live there."

"I *love* accents." She gave me a ravenous look that said *I'll rip off your arms and feed you my pussy,* and bit her lip— oh fucking God, that perfect mouth. Then she moved in so close I could smell her perfume—the expensive sort that's more dry than sweet. Glancing down her body, I could see the cinching on the poppy-print dress—and there were her lickable breasts again. Running her fingers down my arm, she said, "French turns me on."

Eh bien.

Horny as fuck, I snatched hold of her wrist, leaned right in, then put my lips against her ear. "You like me, but how much?"

"Well … the thermometer's rising," she whispered. I felt her exhale, felt her sway towards me, and in return, my clit got so hard it felt like a full-grown cock. I wanted to get it out right then, that metaphysical cock, and fuck her against the wall, fuck my fucking job away, fuck away my smartass one-liners, fuck away this life I'd made—this life that stank of corpses. Her skin, up close, was so fucking flawless, and that scent—I could drown in her.

Suddenly, the red-haired brute shoved his way between us. He smelt of oily meat—burgers with pickles. He must have decided it was his job to police Michaela's flirtations, because he glowered and spoke through his teeth: "You're missing the talk, *Miss*." Then he caught my eye and opened his jacket to flash me his gun.

"Packing steel, are we," I said. "Well, who isn't these days."

That made him growl. "Think you're clever, don't you, Frenchie."

His buddy started to urge him to calm it.

"Nice wit," I told Redhead, who'd gone scarlet with

rage. "Wanna dance?"

He hissed, "If it's the last fucking tango."

"*Vraiment?* Had you down as a *solo* dancer." I hung over the words so he got the hint. As soon as he realized I'd called him a "wanker," he made a noise like a rabid dog and reached for his gun. He was so angry that his *petit ami* had to cut between us, murmuring words of warning: "Mr. Cross wouldn't like it if we started firing right now."

I was thrown, all the same. Why had I been hired to travel to England and kill this hottie at a fancy price, if there were already guns guarding her? Truth is, some fuckheads love life too much to risk the Big Hit. They'll put a bullet in a kneecap, but never through a head. So why would Algernon hire them to watch his wife, when he was the one getting the poison pen letters? There was just one answer. There was something he didn't want Michaela to do. Something he was afraid of.

Somehow, the woman had power.

Grey-haired guy glared down at me. "We don't want no trouble, Miss. Are you going to the talk or not?"

I said I was. After all, I had to go where Michaela went. Plus I knew that Algernon was expecting me, the bitch who'd kiss his wife goodnight. Odette had told him to have Michaela available from six onward. It was just a matter of waiting for Mr. Bigshot to call the guards off and let me work my mojo.

Problem was, I was thinking with my dick instead of my Glock. *Merde, Jae,* I told myself, *this is your final hit—the one you can't fuck up. One bullet, then you're free.*

It was a twisted little book talk, that's for sure. We stood at the back of the room, the guards directly behind us standing so close I could smell the redhead's aftershave. Up front, was Algernon, going on and on about the writing process, standing near a table that was stacked with copies of his latest. I stared at him. I didn't get to see the actual client very often. Odette just told me where to point the gun.

Algernon was unnaturally pale—far paler than he looks in the papers—with small beetle eyes that popped against his paleness. He wore a navy blazer with gold buttons. How very English! How very Lord-and-Lady!

His audience wore elegant dresses and suits—some of the men were even in tuxedos. These were the people who keep furs next to their rifles and eat *fois gras* on tap. The thing I hate most is how these rich bastards so often complain about the crimes of this world, then make everyone's lives a living death.

Now *that's* torture. I'd ask for the bullet every time.

Anyway, at one point during this piece-of-shit book talk (which focused, by the way, on the death threats he'd received, more than the fucking books), Algernon went suddenly quiet and seemed to look right at me, beetle eyes opening so I could finally see the whites. *That's right,* I wanted to tell him. *I'm the bitch you've paid to kill your wife.* But then, I noticed him pluck at his left earlobe. Then, wouldn't you know it, Michaela's guards left the room, their footsteps as soft as thieves'.

When Michaela saw that they'd gone, her cheeks went pink and her eyes flashed and she placed a hand on my arm. I felt electricity connecting between us. Heady stuff. "Want to get out of here?" I whispered. "I'll teach you French if you teach me Hot."

She gave a sultry smile that made the cleverness glint in her pupils. "Would you like to smoke a joint?" she asked.

"Do dogs piss?"

She led me from the room.

Chapter 3

Soon we had our backsides nestled into a couple of cushions on the tiniest balcony overlooking the Surrey hills. I've never been one for the countryside, but the silence was good. Between the concrete posts that lined the balcony, the fields looked so green—same with the trees that hid the main road.

Alors, I was trying to play it cool, with my heart and groin pumping, but even the weed wasn't making me relax. I could smell her skin, the expensive lotions on it, and what I wouldn't have done to run my fingers down her throat and across her ridge of her tits, before reaching under that girly skirt and finding her pussy.

Shit, I'd never killed anyone this alive.

We talked about Algernon's stupid book talk, while I wondered how I'd manage to shoot this beauty. Mostly, killing doesn't give me trouble. (At least, not until the nightmares, the blood you can't stop, the angry corpses with their thick blue tongues …) But I reminded myself that I wanted out of hitting, and somehow this woman with her unforgivable curves was making me realize how badly I needed to leave the game. She made me want to do the opposite of hitting—

to throw myself into the orgy, and rub and thrust and moan.

Bonjour fucking. *Au revoir* blood.

Anyway, Micheala passed me the joint—it had her lipstick on the tip, like a just-kissed cock. I inhaled, then she made me cough mid-drag, because that's when she said, "You're either here to save me or kill me. So, which is it?"

It took me a moment—yeah, Michaela Cross had made me lose the *cool* that Odette had once said no one could crack. After a moment, I replied, "Maybe both."

She glanced down for a moment, and I saw fear flare in her pretty brown eyes. There was the innocent girl I'd seen in the photo. Jesus, I felt like a murderous bitch.

I passed her the joint and she smoked quietly, gazing ahead at nothing. I took her in—that perfect flesh, that beautiful mouth, her faultless body, her fuck-me-now cleavage. A mist of drizzle was now falling on us, dampening her skin, settling tiny beads of water in her gorgeous braided pigtails. She made me want to unravel them, hold them behind her with a single fist, and use them to yank back her pretty head, while I licked her jaw and listened to her gasps. Her dress had sunken down, and her low neckline revealed more of her chest than ever. The flesh that was still covered globed up beneath the material, full and hefty, damp in the rain.

She passed me the joint, then smoothed her dress over her knees. "So he does want me dead then."

"He's an asshole. That's clear."

"Are you going to do it?" she asked, raising her chin.

That defiant look she gave me made me sizzle, it was so hot. I wanted to say, *No, of course I'm not*, but I didn't feel like I had a choice. I made to tell her—well, I don't know what—but she interrupted me with,

"Never mind. It's always turned me on, you know."

"*Quoi?*" I said. "Death gets you hot?"

She nodded. "Having Milton and Cleaves guard me has been exciting, in a way. So many times over the last couple of weeks, I almost seduced them, just so they'd run their pistols down my skin while we fucked." Here eyes were bright and wild now—and Christ, was she making me horny. If this was a last supper, it was peaches and cream.

I shuffled closer to her and ran the side of my index finger down her arm, starting at her shoulder, heading for her wrist. I felt her breath change, felt her lean into my touch. "Listen," I said, "If I'd wanted, I could have shot you by now. I should have been out of here half-an-hour ago, with the mole satisfied—"

"The *mole?*" Her lips were close now, her breath warm.

"My boss sends someone to check I've done the hit."

"The *hit?*" She shuffled towards me and let her fingers trail my thigh through the dress. "Is that … the *kill?*" She said the word like it was a heated climax. "*Kill me,*" she said, pushing her fingers into my hair. Then in a moment, we were kissing, and she tasted to-die-for, like weed and cherries and dry wine. Her body was hot, and when I pressed myself against her, I felt her breasts push onto mine—large and hot and ready. She pulled back, just a little, and said, "Kill me. Kill me good."

"Nope," I said. "You've done it now. Can't kill a woman who kisses like that." And I meant it. She was gorgeous. Her mouth was as sweet as nectar. *Well, good, Jae Steele. At least you're being candid with yourself.*

She kissed me again, hard on the lips for a good, long time, then finally whispered, at my ear, "What'll happen if you don't go through with it?"

"If I don't shoot you? Depends what we do instead."

"Will you have to kill Algie?"

I snort-laughed. "You named him after *pondweed?*"

She flushed, laughing into my eyes, and said, "Suits him, don't you think?" Then her smile fell, and she grew serious. "Since the death threats started," she said, "he's been carrying a gun. And he's got security all over the place— Milton and Cleaves are just the beginning."

Her sharp mind was ripe for crime. Already, she spoke like a pro.

I thought for a minute. If I didn't kill Michaela, I'd have to kill Algernon. After all, if Michaela lived, Odette would find out soon enough. But seeing as she'd already been paid in full, what did she have to lose if Algernon died and Michaela lived? Algernon's death would be pinned on one of the nuts who'd sent him the death threats, and nobody else would even know he'd tried to murder his wife. The only downside for Michaela was being questioned by the cops, but we could cook up a story. God knows, I'd done that before.

So how to hit Algernon? I'd have to make it look like a "death threat" kill—lunatics who wanted to kill rich authors didn't march into their homes and shoot them. That would be risky. And intimate. No, lunatics blew you up with letter bombs or …

An idea hit me. I had that cell phone in my bag—the clever little bomb that Uncle Stan had left me. I could plant it on him. *Oui, d'accord. Ça marche.*

I leaned in close to Michaela again. "Listen, beauty," I said, running my fingers down her collarbone, then across the ridge of her gorgeous tits. "It's either you or him. Okay?"

She bit her lip, thought for a minute, till the lights came on in her eyes. "If someone tries to kill you, you damn well kill them back," she said. Then she leaned towards me, open-mouthed, and licked slowly up my jaw—making every cell of me burn—before playing her tongue over my earlobe, until I was heady with pleasure … "How will you kill him?" she asked.

I told her about the phone, the bomb. Her smile was sloped and sexy.

"You're my knight in shining armor," she said, sultry, at my ear. "You know what that gets you?"

"If your tongue's involved, I'm in."

"Mmm," she said, "come inside and see."

And hit or no hit, I wasn't about to refuse.

Michaela, the fucking goddess. Michaela, the perfect

screw. Even if I tell you how she stripped in front of me, hips rocking slowly, sliding her skirt up over her thighs in a way that made me long to bite them—even if you know how she slid her dress-straps down her arms, revealing the silky black bra underneath, and let her breasts bulge forward as she slid that dress over her hips—even if you know all that, along with the hunger darkening her smile, you can't imagine how alive she was.

I sat on the edge of the bed as she stripped for me, slowly, all lace trappings and swelling ivory flesh. She had the most perfect breasts, so big and full, and her curves were sensational, her ass so big and welcoming ... She rolled the stockings down her legs so teasingly that their thin fabric was suddenly the kinkiest thing in the world, not to mention her pale thighs. I was already out of my dress—I hate wearing those 'lady clothes'—and I played with my clit through my briefs, trying oh-so-hard not to come yet. And once she was rubbing her hands over the lacy bra she was wearing, making me hot as fuck to get my hands on the breasts inside it, I decided to play my own little game. "Tell me why he wants you dead," I said.

"Hmm?"

She let a single bra strap slide over her shoulder. That stopped me for a moment—made me moan, in fact—but it didn't stop me completely. Again I said, "Why does that bastard want you dead."

"Guess," she said. Then she put her fingers in her mouth and suckled them for a minute, letting the other bra strap fall. Her breasts were magnificent, spilling over her lacy bra-cups. My clit hardened. Fuck, I was turned on.

I said, "You've got something on him, I'd say. Something that could damage him. Something about those death threats he's received. They're not from you, are they?"

She laughed at that, before stepping towards me, letting the bra fall to the floor, and allowing me an eyeful of her perfect pink nipples. "No, the death threats aren't from me," she said. "But I do have something on him." She raised my chin with an index finger. Then suddenly, she went serious, lowering her face to mine, looking right into me. "I wrote the books," she said. "The Angel Series. All of them."

I was so surprised it took me a minute to reply. "You're the *author*?"

"And guess whose account the royalties get wired to? And guess who's turned into a snake since fame spread his legs?"

I was amazed. "Why let him take the cred?"

"I used to be shy." She'd married for money, she explained, and just wanted a quiet life, writing what she loved. Fame wasn't her style, back then. "He said he'd give me the royalties and he'd do the publicity."

"Then he turned on you?"

"No royalties," she said, "no advances. *Nada*."

"So you stopped writing for him."

She nodded. "I want a divorce. And to see my books in print. But to get my books published, I'll need an agent, a track record …"

"*Oui, oui, je vois.*" What agent wouldn't leap on Michaela, once she'd come out about writing the Angel series? I wanted to read every one of those books now I knew her story. Who wouldn't?

"So," I said, "he wants you dead because he's worried you'll tell everyone you wrote the books."

"Mmm," she said, dreamily. "I *love* your French." She dangled her boobs in front of me, and I had to cup them, feel the weight of them in my hands, before putting my mouth on them to lick them like an animal, my tongue glossing those hard nipples, slicking up that smooth skin. "If you keep me alive," she said, straddling me, "I'll announce I'm the author. Then I'll give you a share of the money I make."

Jesus, *elle était magnifique!* She was too good to be true. But once Algernon had died, there'd be problems with her scheme …

She paused. "You're only killing my husband, right?"

I raised a dry eyebrow. "Depends if you're hot in the sack."

"Then I'm safe."

Knowing death made her hot, I said, "Maybe."

She gave a dark smile. "Well, seeing as this might be my last-ever screw, I want to ask a favor."

"I don't do favors."

"Even when they make you come?"

I told her to try me.

◇◇◇◇

Algernon, it turned out, liked to be fucked. Michaela produced the proof from their dresser. I was sitting on the bed at the time, stupid with lust, having planted my weapons— phone-bomb and gun—on the bedside table. The framed, fancy mirror from Michaela's dressing table reflected me back as a dirty slut, with the messy hair of a savage, hard little nipples, and a convict's eyes. When Michaela turned around, she had a toy in her hand.

"A cock?" I said. "That's your favor?"

Nodding, she let her stare run over me. "You're gorgeous," she murmured. Then she grinned. "Think how you'll look in it!"

"I always look good, cock or not."

She held up the contraption—a black silicone cock of six or so inches, its leather straps dangling. "I want to be fucked with it," she said, "but he always wants *me* to wear it."

Sacré. "Games change," I said. My temperature was rocketing.

Didn't take me long to get into the thing of course. I soon had Michaela on her back on the four-poster bed, while she rolled about, moaning and rubbing that pussy, begging me to fuck her. Around us, the flowery wallpaper seemed to spin and blur.

But that was nothing compared to what was coming.

Picture this: Michaela on her back, her fabulous breasts lolling as I fucked her—me on my knees, raising her big hips, my black cock thrusting in and out of a pussy so tight that my silicone piece could feel it. No need for lube either. Her juices were sliding out of her, covering my cock so I could see the threads of wetness, not to mention the slicked-up shine. She was moaning and drooling, her head falling from side to side, sometimes putting her fingers into her mouth, sometimes pulling them out and dragging them down her throat and chest, before caressing one of those beautiful pink nipples.

The cock felt like my cock, and I'd forgotten that feeling. That's how long it had been since I'd fucked a girl, like this. The harder I thrust, the more Michaela moaned, her breasts lolling, and the more the silicone pressed on my clit, making it throb and burn.

At one point, I paused, just to be a tease. Then an idea hit me—the answer to a problem. I leaned right forward, over her gorgeous body, one hand pawing a big, soft breast, and murmured, "You know, once he's dead, you can play the poor lost widow, and tell the world you *co*-authored the books." As the wife who'd always been a willing co-author, I explained, she'd have no motive for his murder. Instead, she'd be the shy, loving gal who mourns her protector, and wishes she could hide behind him, like she used to. But loving their books so much, how could she not come out? It was the perfect bullshit story.

She was panting and writhing with pleasure, but her eyes grew wide when she saw what I meant, and she grasped my arm. "You mean ... I can carry on the series, but I won't look like I'd wanted him dead?"

"Right," I said. "His fans will love that." The police

wouldn't suspect her if she was the mourning widow carrying on her husband's work. But if she was the angry wife who'd been robbed of her royalties? That was a motive for murder.

"Fuck me more," she gasped, "oh God, do it more ..."

I kissed her hard on the mouth, before I started fucking her again, watching her head jolt back against the pillows, watching her mouth falling open, her lashes half-hiding the glazed lust in her eyes. "*Yeah*," she started to mew, but it was the sex she was reacting to. "*Oh yeah, yeah, yeah ...*" and she reached her arm up behind her, grasping a handful of pillow, as if she might torpedo off into space.

I paused then, which was hard because my clit was so hungry. She arched back, pushing her pussy onto my dick, begging me not to stop. But I love being the domme. A little too much. "You hid because you didn't want the fame," I said. "But you want to be famous now?"

"I've changed!" she gasped. "I want to own what I've done!"

That made me laugh. "Own *this*, honey," I said. Then I started to fuck her again, hard, my cock filling her up, so she cried out like something wild, her breath breaking up with a horny, gasping panic. "*Yeah*," she cried, "oh fucking god, yeah ..." And I was only thinking about how hot she was, which is why, when she came, bellowing out her pleasure, her yells so long and loud that they bounced off the walls, I came too, in a super-charged burn, my cock thrusting insanely, my clit going off like the bomb in my bag.

Next, we changed position, so that I was sitting on the side of the bed, facing the balcony doors, and she was astride me, riding my black cock. I can't even tell you how hot it was to have her tits in my face. I could pull back and have them bounce like crazy in front of me, filling my vision, or I could lean forward and press my face right into them, clutching at one and feeling its nipple so hard in my hand. And when her momentum increased, I felt it in my cock, her thrusts so violent, her body so gorgeously weighty. "Oh fuck," I told her, "oh God, you feel too good ..."

But Michaela had her hands in my hair and was crying out, arching back, her hips going mad like they couldn't get enough of me, and just when I thought she'd finished, she'd cry out again, and her hips would buck just as furiously, on another howling high. Seeing her eyes all glassy with pleasure and her breasts jolting in my face, sent me into my own climax—a great long burn. My cock—my clit—was pulsing with such heaven that when I finally came to, the room was blurry and I could feel sparks behind my eyes.

"Jesus," I told her, "that was quite a ride."

And just as I was about to tell her she'd just about finished me, and I'd never met any girl who could make me come like that, I felt her fingertips stopping my lips. Above me, her eyes were wide with alarm. "Shh!" she whispered. "My husband!"

Sure enough, when I zoned in, I could hear his voice

outside in the corridor. He was speaking to a servant—that's how he sounded anyway. Even though we couldn't hear the words, his voice had an edge of pure power. "If he finds me," she whispered, already clambering off me, "he'll kill me."

I snorted. "He has to hire professionals for that."

I grabbed my gun from the bedside table, but left the phone-bomb where it was. After all, it was easy to reach for. And a phone on a table—what could be more innocent?

In a moment, I had Michaela on her feet, while I stood behind her, running the barrel of my gun down her throat and chest, letting it linger between her perfect tits. She melted, moaning so loud when my cock nudged her clit. "Tell me you're … gonna kill me … tell me you will …"

If I'd have said, *Yeah, I'm gonna kill you right now*, she'd have had the biggest climax of her life. Truth was, the safety catch was on. I'd have told her, if the door hadn't opened right then.

It was Algernon himself. (*Mon Dieu*, did he look taller in the papers.) Seeing us there, gun and all, he grinned like a greedy cat. But he didn't look Michaela in the eye, of course. "I've told the boys to wait outside," he said. "Free show for them. Besides, they're packing heat."

I snorted. Hearing a posh gent say 'packing heat' is pure Monty Python. But behind my laughter I was wary: If I shot Algernon, at any point, I might have to deal with his armed guards bursting in.

Algernon didn't respond to my laughter. "So this is a perk of your job, I suppose," he asked.

"This *is* the job," I said.

He gave a sly half-smile.

Meanwhile, my mind was racing. The phone on the bedside table to my right could be detonated to go off whenever I wanted. I needed to program it to go off in, say, an hour, and then plant it on him before he left. But how the fuck to do all that when he was fixated on us?

Michaela was saying to Algernon, "Tell me you didn't hire her to kill me ..." But even just saying that made her moan afresh (wow, did this bitch love the whole sex-and-death thing!) and when I touched just the tip of the barrel against her clit, she cried out wildly, grasping my wrist so hard. Michaela Cross—my gunplay girl.

Algernon walked right up to Michaela. Cupping her face, he said, "See what I do with wives who think they run my life?"

But Michaela wasn't interested in Algernon. She wanted the cock between her legs and the gun barrel that was stroking her tits. She fell back against me, groaning, rubbing her cunt on my cock. "Kill me," she moaned, "fucking kill me, Jae ..."

I told him, "Looks like your *femme* doesn't even know you're here."

"Oh, she knows, all right." He turned his back, pulled off his blazer and tossed it on the bed.

I've killed men like Algernon. At the end, they cry like babies.

As I teased Michaela's breasts with the cold steel,

making her shudder and press her cunt against my cock, Algernon brought the chair from in front of her dressing table, turned it around so the seat-back was facing me, before sitting astride it, his erection safely hidden. "Oh Mickie," he said, through a too-sweet smile, and it surprised me that he'd use her nickname at a time like this. "You were a good little wife. Up to a point."

Michaela turned her head towards me, reached back and cupped the side of my face. "You make me so horny," she murmured.

Wanting to hide that Michaela and I were friendly—I was meant to be killing her, after all—I asked Algernon if he knew his wife had a deathwish, but he just glared, arms folded. I licked up the side of Michaela's neck, dragging the barrel across her belly. Fuck, this delicious woman. She was enough to make me explode.

"Stick the gun somewhere better," said Algernon, his voice cold. From his breath, I knew he was touching his cock behind the seat-back. When a mark's hiding in any way, you know you're in control.

"*I'll* decide what I do with the gun," I said.

His brows darkened and he rose from his chair. "Slut, I pay your wages," he spat.

"While *I'm* holding the gun," I said, "*you* pay my everything. And while you're here, maybe I won't put a bullet in your brain."

He glanced towards the door, thinking no doubt to call on his men. So I added, "For now, get your cock out. I want you nice and hard."

Chapter 4

I asked Michaela what she'd like for her last supper, and she said 'anal' with me wearing the cock. I thought Algernon would push to fuck her, but when she said it, he looked like he'd hit gold. So that's how we ended up on the carpet, Michaela on all fours while I thrust into her gorgeous ass. She must have loved anal because her asshole took me easily like it was desperate for cock, like it was made to be screwed. She cried out, "Yeah, yeah, yeah!" (though it sounded more like "Yuh, yuh, yuh!") over and over, as if it was the only word she knew, and every time she cried it a little higher, with a little less breath, until she was so excited that I just knelt still on the carpet, as she rammed herself down onto my silicone piece, making me hopelessly hard and wet.

Meanwhile, I held the gun at her head, tangling it in her hair, or else I ran it down her body, enjoying the sight of the barrel on her skin. I knew I had to program that phone, but I had a feeling my time would come.

Algernon stood in front of Michaela, his trousers at his ankles, yanking at his cock (which was now of considerable size) as he let out voluptuous groans. His eyes were trained on my tits and the cock that was sinking into the wife he'd have me kill; and all of us together were a great heaving engine, all hands and moans and gun and stiff dicks. Fortunately, Michaela came first, her body slamming down on my cock so hard that my own cunt gave way, filling me with an orgasm that kept me pinned high, and didn't end until I felt Algernon's cream hitting my tits.

After he'd let spurt after spurt fly at me, groaning hard the whole time, Algernon walked right up to us, held his sticky cock over Michaela and told her, "Clean it."

Big mistake. He didn't rule this scene.

In moments, Michaela was off my cock and I was facing her husband. "I'm in control here," I told him. Not you."

"You heard her," said Michaela, struggling to her feet. "She's the pro, Algie."

He gestured towards the door. "There's a whole heap of muscle, armed and ready for both of you."

Suddenly, I knew what I had to do. "You know what," I told Michaela, "I'd actually like to see you clean his cock."

She blinked at me, confused. "Well," she said, clearly going with it, "you're the girl with the gun." And Christ, I would have loved to watch my dirty kitten lick the spunk from her would-be killer's cock, but I had to get at that phone— which I did in a second. While Algernon moaned, enjoying Michaela with a gross kind of triumph, I set the detonation on the phone for 1 hour's time. It didn't take a moment—I was in good practice.

Now I just had to plant it.

"You women," groaned Algernon, glancing at me, his hand splayed on his wife's head. "Always checking your fucking phones."

"You men," I said, with a dry slur, "never have the balls to kill your own bitches."

In a flash, an angry Algernon had pulled up his trousers, zipped his flies, and was striding up to me. He grasped one of my slicked-up tits in one hand and pressed his mouth onto mine—a daring move that took me by surprise. He then wiped his hand, gooey from his handling of my breast, across my face. The prick. So I grabbed his fucking arm and twisted it behind his back. He let out moan of pain—but his boys must have thought it was a pleasure-groan, because no one burst in with a pistol. I put my lips against his ear and said, "Listen to me, you piece of shit. Fuck off and let me do my job."

"Fine," he hissed. So I tightened my jujitsu grip. He gasped, then, and let out a fearful "Yes, *Miss!*"

See? They whimper like kids.

"Michaela," I said, twisting Algernon's arm again to make him moan in pain. "Get me your husband's jacket." I gestured towards the bed, where he'd tossed it when he walked in. She grabbed it, brought it over, and held it out. From there, it was easy enough to drop the phone into one of the pockets. "Where are you going now?" I asked him, mouth against his ear.

"To dinner!" he said. I wrenched his arm again,

making him cry out, "*Miss!*"

"He's giving a speech," said Michaela.

"*Another* one?" I asked.

"Please, Miss," he breathed, "let me go! Everyone's waiting."

Bon. This was just what I wanted to hear. Algernon would soon be walking towards a load of smarmy bastards—who, *á mon avis*, had all been as cruel as my parents—with a bomb in his pocket.

Revenge? I like my cold cuts.

I let him go, and Michaela handed him his jacket. "Just remember," I told him, "you hired me through Odette. Dealing with you and your men wasn't part of the deal."

Straightening his shirt collar, he looked like he was about to be witty. But clearly, he knew better, because he gave Michaela the most cursory of looks before leaving the room, his jacket over his arm.

After you've had the climax of your life, there's no point getting your head blown off. Michaela and I couldn't risk going down the stairs—Milton and Cleaves would be hiding in wait with orders that contained the words "kill" and "bitches." So Michaela and I tied the sheets together and threw ourselves over the second-floor balcony.

I thought she'd be scared, but the problem was getting her to stop chuckling. Halfway down, she thought it was a hoot—the adrenaline, *je figure*. Looking up at me, hanging there in her baby-pink leggings and T-shirt that announced "Fight Like a Girl," she looked like a cheating teen, with her red face, watering eyes, and her body convulsing with giggles. I thought we'd never get down at all, let alone without getting caught. But we did—and we made good time.

En fait, we ended up in the parking lot at the back of the house where we had our pick of BMWs and Mercs, but I went for a red convertible with the top left down. (Always steal the car that belongs to a rich kid. They're always *laissez faire*, which makes a thief's job easier.) In this case, the soft-top wasn't only easy to get into, but was also, to Michaela's mirth, easy to drive away. They'd left the keys in the glove compartment, *blague à part*, along with Gucci shades, some Camels, and a zippo lighter. Party.

I reached for the smokes as I drove us through the Surrey hills, the big house disappearing behind us, my new girl beside me and a big fat smile on my big fat face. Me—Jae Steele—with an alleycat grin. Odette: eat your heart out.

I lit two of the Camels between my lips, while Michaela stripped off her T-shirt, letting her glorious tits loose on the world. Topless, she knelt up on the seat and held out her arms, birdlike.

"Cigarette, beautiful?" I asked, offering her a smoke.

But she wasn't listening. She was thrusting her boobs ahead of her, like the figurehead from a ship, throwing back her head and screaming with pleasure. There she was, my new girl, her dark curls streaming behind her, while she whooped at the sun ahead, calling out, "Fuck you Algernon!

Fuck you, you son-of-a bitch!" and "Fuck you Surrey hills! I never liked you anyway!" Then, when her lungs had run out of gas, she laughed into my eyes, the lights in her pupils like exploding sparks. "We'll have to go back, you know," I said, "for appearance's sake."

But she didn't care because it wasn't about that. It was about winning. And Michaela hadn't won for ... well, maybe never.

She took her cigarette, fell back in her seat, and arched her body towards the setting sun. And when I glanced across at her, the sunset—all pink and gold—was throwing soft colors on her bare skin. "You pack such *steel*, Jae," she told me, rolling towards me and exhaling a trail of smoke. "I'm so lucky you came. What'll we do now?"

I was about to tell her we'd have to "*cook up a story*" and "*take you back to the house so you can look like the mournful widow.*" But somehow, I knew she wouldn't do any of that. She was ready for an adventure. A pulp fiction saga, with hold-ups in comic stores and hidden identities. So I said, "If it's murder you're after, count me out. That's my last hit, baby. Killing's been killing me."

"I know," she said, "but aren't there other things we could do? Pickpocketing? Short cons?" Her lips were close to my ear. "Train me," she said. "Go on, Jae! I won't disappoint. And I won't get clingy either. Train me! Come on. When has crime ever let you down?"

Strange. That question again. The universe was whispering.

"You don't need the money," I said.

"I'll invest. Like a business."

"Life isn't easy on the sly," I said.

"Fuck life," she said.

"Fuck *death*," I replied. Then I found myself laughing as the sunset grew amber, throwing its romance over the hills and covering us with its honey. "Fuck death!" I laughed, throwing back my head, tossing my cigarette out of the window.

"Yeah," said Michaela. "Fuck life and fuck death."

And that was just the beginning.

LOVE GUN

FULANI

L o v e   G u n

It's an easy late afternoon drive through desert scenery: a heat haze in the distance, tumbleweed racing alongside her. There are only a few other cars. Although, since she's doing fifty in an elderly campervan, when another vehicle appears in her rearview mirror, it catches up and overtakes her pretty swiftly. A 4x4, heavily loaded, cruises up behind her and overtakes with a turbo growl and a cloud of dust. That's okay. With the age of her van, Cerise has learned to be a patient driver.

Cerise is pleased she's found this road. It's not the route she normally takes, driving home from her parents. The satnav app on her cellphone displayed it, she trusted what it showed her and it's all working out.

As the sky darkens, the highway begins to climb. It twists, snakelike, along the sides of valleys and between bare rock crags. Parts of it don't seem to be up to full interstate standard, just one lane in each direction and narrow shoulders at the roadside. There's a green sign at the roadside, MOUNTWEAZEL 10. Arrow on the sign points straight ahead. The name of the place bothers Cerise for a reason she can't pinpoint.

As the road gains altitude the weather seems to close in. Spots of rain appear on her windshield. There might not have been much traffic earlier, but what there is has turned into a long convoy that seems to be going slower the higher they get.

Slow becomes crawl, and crawl becomes stop.

In her old, battered campervan, Cerise looks out at the taillights in front of her. They've been at a dead stop for about fifteen minutes. Rain's coming down harder now, and the lights become blurred through the windscreen. She switches on the radio in the dashboard, hits a button to activate the traffic news function. This is supposed to allow local traffic broadcasts to interrupt whatever's playing.

Ironically, what's playing is Gary Numan's "Cars". Lyrics about only being able to receive, not transmit; about how his image breaks down; about nothing seeming right. But she's not receiving any traffic news. Nothing to tell her why they've stopped.

She sighs. The easy drive home has suddenly become a difficult one, and while the long straight desert road had begun to relax her, the traffic jam is messing with her mood. The last few days have been a whirlwind of stress. If the jam takes any length of time to clear, it will take something pretty fucking magical to lower her stress levels.

People around her have switched off their engines. Some get out of their cars and peer at the waterlogged sky, at the crags above the highway and the growing line of vehicles, and then back at the sky.

Cerise kills the ignition on her van.

In front of her is the 4x4 that passed her earlier, says on the tailgate door it's a "Barbarian". The guy who gets out of it could be a barbarian too. Leather trousers. Leather flying jacket. Long hair. He'd look good riding a horse with a broadsword strapped to his back and his hair flying in the wind. Except he pulls a hat out of his car to protect himself against the rain. Oddly in view of his clothes, it's a top hat. He has a brief conversation with the driver of the truck in front of him. Then he turns, walks to the rockface beside the blacktop and shimmies up thirty feet or so, to where there's a solitary tree perched at the top of the crag. He stands there, looking out as if surveying some unmapped, unknown territory.

Cerise suddenly feels dowdy. The guy looks like he's a performer. Maybe he does fire-eating or knife-throwing or bullwhip tricks at festivals. Maybe he lives a commune and has perverted sex with a dozen partners at a time. She, meanwhile, is driving back from seeing her parents. They live in a small town, are in their seventies and are no longer in the best of health. She's had to spend a week playing nurse. Her jeans have holes in the knees. Her top is a man's dress shirt, worn outside the jeans and coming to mid-thigh, and her fleece is the one she wears for gardening. Oh, and her bra and panties don't match and neither is exactly new.

Her mind fixates on the idea of the guy wielding a bullwhip. Projecting his power, snake-like, and wrapping it around her body. A seductively scary mind's-eye picture. One that makes her toe tremble on the brake pedal.

Cerise pulls on the handbrake, climbs out of her van. She has a feeling she might be about to burst her mental bubble. He intrigues her, but she knows he might not be as exotic or erotic in real life as she imagines. She might as well know the worst.

She sighs, pulls the fleece more closely around her and follows him up the crag. It's an easier climb than she expected, just moving from one boulder to another.

She justifies her action in a dozen different ways. He might have heard what's going on and how long they'll be stuck. She wants to see him close up, because of the leather trousers. The attraction is having known bikers and Goths when she was younger, a few guys on the fetish scene since then. She wonders if there's a better view of what's causing the traffic jam from up there. She needs to stretch her legs. She's bored. The other seven reasons are gradations of visceral urges, based on fire-breathing and knife-throwing and bullwhips.

Cerise reaches the tree. She expects it to be stunted and windblown. Instead it's a big, old gnarly thing. The guy's standing under the dark tracery of its branches. They give some shelter from the rain. His gaze doesn't seem set on any one place. Almost like he's looking into the past, the future, or an alternate universe. But he turns and nods at her. It's a casual acknowledgment of what they have in common— membership of this suddenly non-traveling community.

His top hat appears to have a set of welders' brass goggles strapped around them. Being a top hat, it makes him look tall. Cerise feels smaller than she really is—though perhaps it's not just the top hat. He has something else about his bearing that seems larger than life.

Despite the drizzle there's a tang of diesel exhaust hanging in the air from the stalled highway. A smell Cerise interprets as a combination of fire, oiled metal and whips.

"The truck driver says it's a major incident," the guy says. "Something about a landslide. They're thinking it may not be cleared tonight."

That would make sense. Cerise notes that the opposite, eastbound lane is empty of traffic. She can't see more than a dozen cars ahead of her campervan, though, as the road follows the contour of the crag and disappears from view. The landslide isn't visible. There are no flashing blue lights in the distance. All around them, the rain has dissolved colors and washed out details. It's as though they're in a bubble separated from the rest of the world by a couple of dimensions.

"Does it matter that you won't get where you're heading today?" she asks.

He shrugs. "I was heading for Mountweazel." He points to a faint yellow criss-cross glow of lights in the distance, where the line of hills gives way to flat land. From where they are it might as well be an alternate universe away.

"So near, yet so far. By the time I get there, the thing I'm going to will be pretty much over. I'll say hi to a couple of people, probably, and be heading straight home again. And I can't get a cellphone signal, so I can't let them know I won't be there."

Then he asks Cerise the same question.

She shrugs. "I'm just on my way home. Guess it doesn't matter what day I get there." She leaves unsaid that she hadn't been on any kind of adventure.

"It's just as well I'm in the camper," she continues. "I can make tea and coffee. Even cook a meal." She was going to say "make up the bed and sleep" but maybe that would have sounded a little forward.

His smile is wolfish enough that Cerise wonders if she should have worn a red hooded cloak.

It's still in the wardrobe at home. She didn't imagine she'd have an occasion to wear it on this trip.

In the campervan. They sit facing each other on the two seats in the back, a small table fitted on a stalk that slots into the floor. He puts his top hat on the luggage rack above the front passenger seat. The kettle's beginning to boil. The rain is drumming on the roof. She gently probes his personality and his business. His name is Ragnar. He says it's his real name, his mother is Swedish.

Cerise is a nickname she acquired in her teens, but it's more part of her identity than her real name these days. She doesn't bother to explain that to Ragnar.

By then the kettle's boiled and she makes coffee.

They drink and talk.

"By day," Ragnar says, "I'm a freelance IT nerd. But business flatlined, and I got into making stuff with my hands. You know about steampunk? Things that look like old Victorian gadgets made with steam pistons and cogwheels? I make things like that."

Cerise nods. She reads and web-surfs enough to know steampunk exists, that it's an outgrowth of Goth and some other cultural trends. A reinvention of the past as way of coping with the present. A style that goes back into the future. It explains the top hat, the flying jacket, the dress shirt, the leather trousers. The *brown* leather trousers, which seem to Cerise like a waste of good leather. Brown is part of the steampunk colorway—it's all brass and brown, gray and tin. Among the bikers, Goths and fetish people she's known, if it wasn't black it didn't count as real leather.

"There's a steampunk convention in Mountweazel," the barbarian continues. "I am—or I was—going there as a trader. My designs make good money."

"What's your best product?"

"They're all one-offs. But some designs I like better than others. My favorite's the Enhanced Mesmeric Affection Projector."

"The *what?*"

"Let's just call it a Love Gun."

The amused expression on Cerise's face prompts Ragnar to mumble "I'll be back in a minute".

While he's gone, Cerise contemplates the Ultimate

Meaning of Life, the Hand of Fate and the Mystickal Significance of the land itself slipping sideways to trap her on the road with a leather-clad steampunk craft-worker called Ragnar. There's no news about when the road will be reopened, just rumors passed from driver to driver. The darkness and rain places them in a bubble outside the real world. As does the lack of a cellphone signal. The reason they met was because they simply happened to be moving in the same direction at the same time when the earth decided to move. Or maybe that "simply happened" phrase masks something more than coincidence?

Cerise has a partner. They've been together eight years. They've done a lot of kinky stuff together. Everyone has fantasies, don't they? Cerise's fantasies run from the banal to the hardcore. Being tied to a bed and licked by many tongues (yes, happened). Dressing as a whore and arranging to meet her partner on a disused industrial estate, where he can fuck her against a chain link fence (he tied her to it, it was pretty wild). A *Story of O* type scenario involving being taken in chains to a place where she experiences repeated punishment and violent sex, as part of a slave training program that runs for weeks and stretches beyond every psychological limit she has (Cerise is pretty sure she doesn't want to do that one for real, though; or at least, one evening of it would be enough). But there's no political correctness about fantasies. The subconscious doesn't censor.

Oh, and she and her partner aren't monogamous. They've done threesomes and moresomes, they've been to a swingers' club a few times and they're both had affairs. Though recently—not so much. The usual stuff has slowed them down. Life, his work, her parents' illnesses. They're in danger of becoming normal and boring.

She figures when she gets home she'll tell her partner what happened, explain the situation and use her sexual skills and submissiveness to seek his forgiveness. But for all she knows, being here with Ragnar is just a way for the universe to give her partner space and time to have a one night stand of his own. And if that's the case, she wonders what fantasy of his that might fulfill.

The Love Gun comes in a metal case, the kind that's used to protect fragile things from airport baggage handlers. When Ragnar pulls it out, it looks like an oversized flintlock pistol with extra gadgets bolted to it. The muzzle ends in something like a small satellite dish—or a colander—with an array of magnets and antique valves inside it. Along the top of the muzzle is a tiny single-piston engine, maybe a model steam engine. Cerise marvels at the craftwork on it: intricately carved brass and highly polished wood. Where the crankshaft slots into the bore, the opening of the bore is delicately shaped to resemble a woman's lips.

Dials on the wooden stock are labeled "Proclivity" and "Intensity", with scales marked in miniature Roman numerals.

"It is actually steam-driven," Ragnar explains. "There's a water reservoir and a small gas burner that drive a tiny generator, enough to power the electronics on it. But that all takes half an hour to set up, and fortunately it'll also work off a couple of batteries that fit into the handgrip." Then he hands her a small booklet out of the box.

The Device draws on the ground-breaking work of Franz Anton Mesmer in the field of Animal Magnetism, developed in conjunction with the Techniques of Dr. S. B. Smith and others who worked on the use of Electricity in the cure of Hysterical and other conditions. It incorporates modern understandings of Electro-Magnetic Field Applications along with heretofore Unpublished and Undisclosed Military Research on the Dispersal and Reintegration of Brain-waves, themselves based upon Study of the Practices and Higher Awareness of certain Oriental Mystics.

There's more, an elaborate spoof treatise on the supposed workings of the device that make Cerise chuckle.

"You're not taking the explanation very seriously," Ragnar remarks, one eyebrow raised sardonically.

"It's wonderfully written. But practical proof of its effectiveness? That's another thing entirely. You'd have to use it on me."

"Very well." He slips two batteries into the handgrip. She notices even the batteries have been specially decorated, with wood veneer sleeves around them. He points the Love Gun at her and she gravely watches the flickering antique valves inset into the satellite dish end of it. The valves are purely for show, as far as she can see—they're just an elaborate setting for small LEDs.

"You won't feel the results instantly," Ragnar says.

"It can be anything up to half an hour before the Love Gun shot takes effect."

There's something deeply absurd, Cerise feels, about two adults sitting in the back of a campervan playing with what is, while very finely made, basically a toy or roleplay prop. It's absurd enough that she can feel laughter trying to spill from her mouth.

And yet it's serious, too. As serious as any other social symbol: a cross, a pentagram, a wedding ring (she doesn't wear one, her partnership isn't a marriage), a slave collar (she has one friend who wears one). It's a physical device that has no intrinsic "power", but can be used to define the nature of a relationship.

"Now try it on someone else. Someone who doesn't know you've fired it at them." Cerise is assuming of course that because it's a toy, this will have no effect whatever. And Ragnar seems amused by the idea. He comes over to Cerise's side of the van, the driver's side. He opens the window and leans out, looking for a suitable target.

"Two cars back. The couple in the little red hatchback."

He hefts the Love Gun. Lights blink and she can see, now, the piston moving back and forth between those carefully-tooled lips. Then he closes the window.

"Done."

So now they're sitting next to each other. The sofa is the top of a slippery slope of seduction. It's just a question of who makes the move that lets sexual gravity pitch them into erotic freefall.

The universe does. There's a spear of lightning that illuminates the van as clearly as a camera flash. For a fraction of a second they're overexposed, stark in black and white. The thunder crash (whip crack?) is simultaneous, and strong enough to rock the van on its suspension.

Cerise's head is in Ragnar's lap, hands protectively over her head and his hands protectively over hers.

Cerise isn't a jumpy person, isn't afraid of storms, isn't easily alarmed. But that was a bit close.

"The lightning just took out the tree we were standing under," Ragnar says, astonished.

There's a weird creaking sound, and the road bounces under them again.

She doesn't take her head away from his lap.

"That was the tree trunk keeling over." From the way his thighs and stomach move, Cerise guesses he's looking out of the window. "It came halfway down, but it looks like it's stuck between a couple of big rocks. I don't think it's coming any further."

Coming down. Going down. Her face is pushing harder against his groin. The power of suggestion?

He doesn't seem to have any issues with her head being in his lap. Judging by the flex of his thighs, the warmth that penetrates through the leather, the real issue is whether what's under the leather has to stay tightly wrapped in there, or gets to come out and play.

Small voice, Cerise's: "Did you say you had a

partner?"

"I didn't say anything. And yes, I do have a partner. But we don't have a normal relationship."

Well, that's not surprising. No one Cerise knows has a normal relationship. Deviant is the new normal. The only exception, Cerise thinks, is her own relationship. It started out kinky but gradually achieved its own level of subdued deviancy. Pressures of work, family commitments and other "normal" reasons played their part in that. Though they had managed those few days in Montana, six months ago …

"Oh?"

Ragnar smiles. Probably. She can't see his face from down there.

"My partner moonlights as a pro Domme. Even as we speak, she's applying a cane to some poor guy's ass and he's paying her for the privilege."

"Ah, but that's not sex, is it?"

"True, it's not. But when she's done, she'll call her girlfriend and they'll have some quality strap-on time together."

Much as Cerise's partner has had one night stands when he's been away from home, and much as she can go with the mystical-universe-creating-opportunities approach, she suspects the truth is more prosaic. Her partner is probably taking the opportunity of her absence to catch up on work.

Oh well. It's not like they have a normal relationship anyway. Not like they've *had* a normal relationship, anyway, despite current trends. Which should, ideally, be reversed.

Like steampunk, the way to go forward is to go back. To recover their old spirit of deviance.

What she's doing now is giving her the anticipation of wickedness. It could be the kickstart she and her partner needed. It teases her, little electrical quivers up and down her limbs. Almost like the lightning flash left a residual current crackling around her.

Cerise had switched a light on, a small LED reading lamp above the sofa. She doesn't want what she's about to do to be illuminated.

She asks Ragnar to push the button. When he does, she rolls over so her head is still in his lap but now she's facing up towards him.

His hand rests on her left breast as though that's the most natural place in the world for it to be. She reaches up with her right hand, toys with his long hair. His fingers push into the fabric of her shirt and bra, finding and circling her nipple.

"That would feel better if I didn't have clothes in the way."

Ragnar obligingly unbuttons her shirt. His fingertips are surprisingly hot as they track down her cleavage, sternum, stomach, navel. With difficulty, Cerise props herself up on one elbow and unfastens her bra one-handed. He helps her remove both shirt and bra. As she lies back down, the fingers of his right hand gently pinch at her nipples while his left hand rests under her belt buckle, palm against her skin and fingertips grazing the top of her panties. Cerise knows her sudden short gasps of breath give away her excitement. Feverishly she undoes the buckle of her jeans, the zip. Raises her feet so Ragnar can pull off her boots, and curls her spine to get her ass far enough off the seat that she can remove her jeans.

And her panties. She's grateful the darkness hides its mismatch with her bra.

The connections in her head are firing faster than lightspeed. Given her own tendencies, there's a warp factor involved. Her brain serves up images she's seen, fantasies she's always had, fantasies she's scared to have, things she's done in the past, things she's talked about with her partner but they've never done.

Being naked with a random, clothed, male barbarian stranger is exciting but also disturbing in a good way. Exciting, because sex is going to happen. Disturbing, because his clothing and her nudity is a marker for her submission—and she doesn't yet know what kinds of desires he might enact on her body. Doesn't know what she's submitting to.

His right hand is back on her breast. He drags his nails lightly across the flesh, a thrilling hint of peril. Fingers of his right hand crawl delicately between her legs, which she parts. One finger scoops gently inside her, finding lubrication there. He moistens and then presses the button.

"Do you find," she says teasingly, "your Love Gun always works this well?"

"Always," he replies solemnly. "It's surprising, but it creates an impressive psychological effect. Call it mesmerism.

Or call it a placebo, an excuse to let unconscious desires surface ... You do have unconscious desires, right?" All the time his fingers are gently squeezing her nipple and working around her clit.

There's any number of progressive small graduations of sexual pleasure. They start with possibilities, then intention, then anticipation. They progress to first touch, first button or zipper, and being naked enough to fuck; they include the being-in-the-moment of visual stimulation, smell, taste. She's looking up at Ragnar's face, shadowed in the night. But she can see the concentration in his eyes, the pupils darker and more infinite than the sky. She can smell the richness of his brown leather trousers, more complex and sensuous than any of the black motorcycle or fetish clothing she can remember.

Then she's rolling over, reaching for what turns out to be a button fly on his trousers. Ragnar starts to unbutton his shirt and she shakes her head.

"Not necessary." Cerise wants to preserve the dynamic. The symbolism of being nude with a man who's still dressed. She can already access the one piece of skin she needs. The sensitive erectile tissue. Licks her lips and wipes them across the tip of his ...

There's metal against her teeth.

"It's called an ampallang."

Cerise's brain does a sideways slide via *fang* to *vampire*.

"You can bite me later."

Then she's running her tongue around the head of his cock, exploring the piercing. Wondering how it'll feel inside her. Liking the red wine taste of it and thinking that his red wine and her honey are a good match.

And it occurs to her she's got his cock in her mouth and she hasn't even kissed him. Oh well.

The van isn't that small, but with the folding table in place there isn't a lot of space for her to slip off the sofa and kneel between his legs. The move requires contortion of limbs. It feels, just a little bit, like bondage. Not bondage with ropes, but mental bondage. Her partner tried it once: required her to pose on her knees, spine erect, arms folded behind her with left hand on right elbow and vice versa, head tilted slightly backwards. Mouth open. And *of course* he'd used her mouth, plastered his cum over her face—after he'd pulled and teased her nipples and slapped her breasts. She'd held the position, though, being the perfect slave for him.

She'd learned other positions too. On her knees, forehead to the floor, ass in the air, knees spread and arms extended to either side. Standing with ankles wide apart and hands behind her head. Her partner had been going through what they later described as his John Norman period, reading the series of Gor novels—and taking notes. There were even websites with infographics to illustrate the slave positions, with names for each. It had been fun, but there was a limit to how far it was possible to take that stuff without becoming obsessive and (hah!) fetishistic about it. She occasionally enjoyed floating around the house on a summer's evening wearing nothing but a silk scarf around her hips and a chunky ankle bracelet, being a willing sexual servitor. But with time, they'd become less hung up on the positional thing. These days they were more eclectic and freestyle on the increasingly rare occasions when they played.

For the purpose at hand, though—for the man at hand—the on-her-knees, arms-behind-back and cock-in-mouth position is the one Cerise adopts. Submission to a stranger is one of her continuing and strong fantasies, acted out and reinforced through the pose.

Ragnar's not a porn star, not instantly and enormously responsive. For the moment at least, it's not a problem taking the whole of him in her mouth. She appreciates that he's completely shaven and there are no hairs tickling the end of her nose. In fact he's more smoothly shaven than Cerise is herself, since she only takes a razor to her skin for holidays, high days and play sessions. She moves her tongue around the cock, exploring the hardness of the ampallang. She sticks out her tongue, using it to stimulate his balls and the base of his cock until she gets a pulse of reaction. Then she puts her tongue back into her mouth, closes her lips tight and applies suction.

"Hold me," he whispers hoarsely. "Use your hands."

Cerise has mixed feelings. Her way of showing submission is to have her hands behind her, as if they were tied. Ragnar's demand is that she should submit in an entirely different way. And there's a logic to it: submission entails doing what's demanded *because* it's demanded, not just because she's restrained and it's going to happen anyway.

She uses her right hand on his shaft, alternating long strokes that rely on saliva for lubrication and a tight grip with thumb and index finger squeezing the base. At the same time her left hand alternates between gentle strokes of her fingernails across his balls, pressure from her thumb at the very bottom of the thick vein on the underside of his cock, and massage of his perineum with index and middle fingers. She keeps it slow, building the tension. And it works. There's no way, now, she can fit all of the cock into her mouth. Not even if she pushes down, accommodating its length in her throat.

Ragnar begins to groan like he might come soon. His thigh muscles tense up.

Cerise disengages her mouth long enough to speak one word.

"Condom?"

He nods.

Sucking Ragnar off is all very well, but when Cerise wants sex and it's going to be a one-off experience, she wants it to be a proper sex experience. In her view, "proper" means penetration.

She points to the overhead locker and he presses the catch on it. A couple of little square packets spill out, each with the telltale ring shape on it. They're not there because she needs them with her partner, and they're not there because she expects to go away alone in the van and need them. They've been there for six months or so, left over from an episode that involved her, her partner, another couple and a weekend in the backwoods of Montana.

There's other stuff in the locker too. A vibrator (the batteries are probably dead by now), some bondage tape, lube, a blindfold, a set of nipple clamps. All part of that same Montana episode. She thinks about suggesting the clamps, but they'd take her out of the immediacy of the moment.

Some journeys are measured in inches rather than miles. In this case, around nine inches. Psychologically, the first inch is the deepest. It's the one from which there is no return. The others are progressive openings up of desire.

Cerise certainly feels opened up. She half-sits and half-lies on a sofa, feet propped against the one opposite. Ragnar kneels on the hard carpeting between the sofas. Kneels between her spread legs. Starts slow and controlled, eyes locked onto hers in the semi-darkness. Her jaw twists, mouth opens in a silent moan. His cock moves harder and faster inside her. She moans quietly and feels self-conscious about it. There are other people parked just a few feet away.

The cock, though, is a transport of delight. It rocks her back and forth, a swaying and swooping that ramps up to the intensity of flying on the back of a dragon.

Why a dragon? The most exotic thing she's ridden, for real, is a camel. Then she gets it, makes the connection. When she's lying in bed at home, there's a print of a Chinese dragon on the wall. Bed, sex, Chinese dragon. Sex, therefore dragon. Dragon taking her out of herself, letting her spirit free.

And the ampallang moving within her is like the rasp of dragon's teeth.

Here there be orgasms, as old maps didn't ever say.

Dragon sets her belly alight.

She bites down hard on her lip to avoid making too much noise, but ends up whispershrieking: "Oh fuck oh fuck oh fuck." Then gasping for air like the sex has used it all up.

There's a time out of time that's just filled with their breathing, the sound of Cerise's abdominal muscles quivering, the silent thunder of their thoughts. Nothing outside the campervan exists.

Eventually something outside the campervan does exist. There's a *whump-whump* of helicopter rotor blades from overhead. As to whose helicopter it is, police or air ambulance or a TV company, there's no telling. The noise fades away, moving in the direction of the landslide, or the fracture in reality, or whatever it was that stopped the traffic.

"What's the time?" Cerise finally asks.

There's a flash of light. Ragnar's very un-steampunk watch.

"Half past one."

Cerise gasps. "We've been stuck here almost five hours?"

"I was reading something recently about one in China that went on for several days. And one in Russia that wasn't cleared for almost a week."

She smiles. "You're telling me we have time to do this all over again?"

Even though she can't see it, she just knows there's an evil smirk on his face.

"I suppose I am. Or we could do *this* instead."

His tongue warm on her vulva, moving around it. Cerise is briefly self-conscious about not having shaved but he doesn't care. His long hair tickles her thighs. Having come earlier, she's not sure she'll reach another climax, but the sensations are interesting. Definitely some endorphin-raising response there. He takes his time, moving across and around each square millimeter of skin as though it was an erogenous zone in its own right. It's hypnotic. Especially when he reaches her labia, delicately tracing up and down each one a dozen times before parting them to reveal her clit. It feels like she's been stripped bare all over again.

"You said something," he murmurs thickly, "about me being a vampire. You wanted me to bite you."

"Hmmm? Yeah, maybe. Ahhhh!"

Ragnar has gripped her clit gently between his teeth. Cerise catches her breath, intimately aware of how exposed she is, how restrained he's being and how her delicate flesh is captured by his strength. It's unnerving and exciting at the same time.

Especially when he pulls at her clit just enough to let her know who's in charge. He searches for, and finds, the boundary between pleasure and pain. Toys with her, eliciting little twisted-lip gasps and open-mouthed moans. Then without releasing his grip he uses his tongue against her clit to give it pressure and heat.

When he finally does loosen his grip, the sensation is as explosive as the bite itself. Cerise still has the vampire image in her head; for a few short seconds she's right there, in the fantasy that comes with the image. A willing victim, a sexual prey.

The idea is only reinforced by his tongue moving inside her, the length of it licking and lapping like a wave. Licking, a tiny part of her brain says, like he's been taught by a lesbian. Not that she's ever likely to find out …

There's a reason it's called *eating her out*. Her thighs are stretched, she's as exposed as a meal on a plate. Carnivorous sex. The kind where she doesn't know whether to pull away or push forward.

She flexes her ass muscles and pushes forward.

Tremors in her pussy, belly, chest. A *what the fuck?* moment before the understanding drops into place that he's reciting something and the words are echoing through her body. Which has already been hollowed out by his cock and reverberates like a huge cavern.

Way, way back in her past Cerise went to a concert where two trumpets were playing in an old church, and the echoes off the high ceiling created a combination tone. So it sounded like there were three trumpets. What's happening inside her pussy is a similar thing, the tones of Ragnar's voice echoing, colliding and multiplying. What's happening is like three-way, four-way, more-way cunnilingus. There's the sense of speaking, being spoken through, in many tongues; of possession, urgency, rapture. The need for ...

... Ragnar uses his fingers. But not in her pussy: he finds the sweet spot just above her pubic bone, about a third of the way between clit and navel, and drives three fingers of his right hand down hard, boring into muscles tensed to resist him. It's a trick she's experienced before, but it's a good one. The clitoris is a surprisingly large organ of which only a small part is normally stimulated. The pressure drives down on it from above, multiplying sensation.

The pressure creates the need for ...

Creates the conditions for ...

Pushes her over the edge of ...

Orgasm.

"What. The. Fuck. Was. That?"

The spaces between her words aren't for emphasis. They're a consequence of Cerise still trying to catch her breath, a full five minutes after the aftershocks of her climax have drained away like an outgoing tide.

"What was what?"

"The words. The poem. Whatever you were saying."

"The Epic of Airship Angelica. It's a long poem, a modern steampunk epic that's a cross between Beowulf and Eskimo Nell. It was the bit where Angelica's captured by an airship pirate. He ravishes her but she fucks him to death and takes over as the new pirate captain."

Cerise manages a quarter of a chuckle. "That's

wrong in so many ways."

"How so?"

It's a while before she has the breath to reply.

"You may purport to be a bit of pirate, but you're in my van, you don't have a crew for me to take over and you haven't quite fucked me to death yet."

Ragnar laughs. "You mean you're still expecting more?"

"I didn't say that ..."

"But you meant it, though."

Cerise giggles. "Gimme ten minutes."

Ragnar reaches into the overhead locker, pulls out a condom packet. And the nipple clamps fall into his lap.

The damn nipple clamps.

"Let me guess. You've conveniently not mentioned your van is also a mobile dungeon?"

"Well ..." Well, it's not. Not exactly. But when she makes up the bed, which involves putting planks between the seats and rearranging the sofa cushions, there are finger-holes in place of handles to lift the tops of the under-seat storage compartment. And those finger-holes can also be used as anchors for bed restraints. Not, of course, that she explains any of this because he'd only insist on trying them out on her. Just like she hasn't explained that the clamps have been in the locker for the last six months, unused since the foursome she and her partner had in Montana.

The clamps are clover-style, with sprung hinges that

mean the more you pull on the chain that connects them, the tighter they grip. And they're tight anyway because Cerise has comparatively large nipples.

"Is there anything else in the locker I should know about?" He puts one hand in there and comes out with the bondage tape. Cerise can see cogs engaging in his brain and steam leaking from his ears.

"I can sense a plan coming together," he says. She doesn't resist as he leans forwards, fingers pressing on the clamps to open their jaws. She draws in breath sharply as he gently locks clamps to nipples. It's been a while. But it's a good pain.

Ragnar hooks a finger around the chain and starts to draw her down on the floor of the van. She hangs back, to see how hard he's prepared to make the clamps tighten.

"*Fuck fuck fuck fuck ...*" under her breath. Yes, he's prepared to pull hard enough to give her some serious ouchies.

"You think I don't know about clamps?" he asks.

A few seconds later Cerise is kneeling on the floor, head between the driver and passenger seats and ass in the air. She senses a moment of being *made ready, assuming the position*. Even though she doesn't yet know what he's planning to do to her that requires the position. Her body's buzzing with anticipation.

Arms pulled up behind her back, so she has to rest her body weight on one cheek. Plastic around her wrists— the bondage tape, of course.

"Now then," Ragnar murmurs, "I'm guessing there's some … Yes, there is."

"Some what?" With her face pressed into the carpet, Cerise's voice sounds muffled and meek.

"Some lube. Because you've had me in your mouth and in your pussy, so that leaves a third hole for me to possess you completely."

Cerise makes a surprisingly kittenish noise. She finds her thigh muscles twitching and ass waggling.

He places a proprietary hand on her ass-cheek. "I see you're excited by the prospect of being sodomized."

It's not her favorite form of sex, but every once in a while—especially if it's part of a connected sequence of sex play, like, now—it has a certain attraction. It's a power thing, a submission thing. Someone asserting control over her body and using it in a perverse way. The mental high is stronger than the physical sensation. Usually.

She shivers when the slither of cold lube hits her asshole.

"I haven't done this for a while. Please be gentle."

That makes him chuckle.

"That sounds so cute. But I've never yet had a woman say it to me and mean it."

There's the brief sensation of the head of his cock pushing hard against muscle, then it's in and filling her.

Slow movements, acute angle. Cerise wriggles—and is reminded of the clamps, because he still has one hand on the chain, pinning it to the floor, and her trying to pull forward yanks hard on her nipples. Hard enough to make her whimper. Hard enough to be agonizingly pleasurable. Ragnar shifts his stance slightly and then it feels like the end of his cock is hitting her clit from the inside. The question flashes into her mind, *is that anatomically possible?* But then the question doesn't matter, because it seems to be happening anyway.

And she's transported. Again.

When she looked out over the traffic jam it seemed to be in its own dimension outside the world, but she and Ragnar were there with hundreds of other people. When he fucked her, she was in a state of rapture but still self-conscious enough to worry about whether she was being loudly rapturous. Now, though, everything outside her own skin is immaterial. She has a cock inside her, pounding her ass. She has the clamps distending her nipples. She has the immanent and immediate knowledge of her submission, of power exercised over her body. She has the weirdness of feeling physical sensations driven by the fantasy in her head. Her clit being mashed in a way that may or may not be physically possible and even the mental image of the damn ampallang, its two small metal balls like teeth gnawing her from the inside. That couldn't be a real sensation, could it, because her ass surely wasn't sensitive enough to feel his piercing? It must be her imagination.

The sense of connection between her mind and body, though, is hypnotically two-way. The things she feels trigger memories, associations, images, symbols, fantasies. But those things also tell her what she's feeling; they create sensation in her body. It's a vicious, volatile, exotic, erotic circle.

The pull on her shoulders and tightness around her wrists: *he's in control.*

The first time she tried bondage, it was a tie that cinched her at the wrists and elbows, and the rope was arranged in a way that pulled back on her shoulders and made her breasts more prominent. It was the first time she'd known she really was helpless, not just play-acting helplessness. It had startled her to find that helplessness was also a form of freedom. Freedom from social restraints. Freedom to enjoy whatever sex was performed on her body. She'd been hooked as badly as any drug; bondage and loss of control were both foreplay and amplifiers of sensation.

The roughness of the carpet against her face: *you submit to this degradation.*

Cerise hadn't always been into degradation. But once she'd embraced bondage, the fantasy of being a captive was a logical step. And captives needed to have their powerlessness enacted upon them and to be forced to enact it. She'd licked shiny leather boots, eaten from a bowl, been tied in positions that displayed her ass and pussy for flogger, cane and cock. Been left in such positions for an hour or more until her partner decided it was time to use her. Anticipation and exposure along with reinforcement of control: the whole experience left her hot and wet. Memory: the first time she'd assumed such a position voluntarily, placing handcuffs on herself, to be ready for her partner when he came home.

The bite of the clamps every time he slams into her ass: *your pain is his pleasure*.

Reading the Marquis de Sade, she'd found a long passage that argued women should be fucked in the mouth and the ass exclusively, never the pussy. His point was to prove that domination and male sexual gratification did not require a pussy. What male sexual gratification did require, for de Sade, was the chastisement of the female. Pleasure comes from perversity and perversity is a pleasure in itself. What de Sade had never figured was that women like Cerise could take pleasure from pain. The nipple clamps were a symbol of that, a symbol that squeezed pain into her body.

The sensation of him moving in her ass: *his possession of you is complete*.

Ass play for Cerise had always been a form of edging—nearly but not quite making her come. She'd needed something more, a vibrator or finger on her clit, to come when her partner was fucking her ass. She'd always been required to ask for it, too. But Ragnar's motive was symbolic in a different way; complete possession meant taking all three holes, one after the other.

He's in control: but that's her guilty pleasure.

You submit to this degradation: the act of submission excites her, her duty and challenge is to enjoy the abuse. There is a track called "Enjoy the Abuse" by an industrial Goth band. It was playing in a fetish club she and her partner went to once. For a while it became the soundtrack of their play sessions.

Your pain is his pleasure: the clamps, obviously, and learning to enjoy the suffering and distress they create when she moves. Because he's holding the chain between the clamps while the force of his cock bounces her whole body and pulls the clamps tighter at every stroke. Meanwhile the sense of being excavated by his cock isn't exactly painful but it electrifies her clit like lightning strikes, making her hips twist and flex, her body twitch and jump and her clit glow and throb.

His possession of you is complete: there's a sudden pulse, discharge, long-drawn-out gasp, and he half-collapses against her buttocks. But that motion, just that last thrust, tips her over the edge.

The pounding of blood in her ears, the sharp gasps of breath, the muscle burn and the exquisite ache of sex gradually recede. The world outside her body eventually comes back into focus.

"Ohh … *fuck!*"

"Surely not again?" Ragnar's voice from somewhere above her. And there's a smell of coffee.

"I took the liberty of brewing up again," Ragnar tells her.

Cerise struggles to get her body upright. She's facing away from Ragnar, and waggles her wrists to signal that she won't be able to drink coffee with them tied.

"Sure. And should I take the clamps off you as well?"

He does the clamps first, bending down behind her

and supporting her spine against his knee. One hand firmly clasped over her mouth while removing them with the other.

"MmmmmPHHHHH!" Cerise bucks against his knee and screams into his hand. She's grateful for the hand that gags her, because otherwise she'd be waking up the entire traffic jam.

"Yeah, I know. They're painful initially, but that's nothing compared to how they feel when they come off. I'm not a complete innocent, I have used them before ..." That phrase, "complete innocent", is so inappropriate it makes her smile.

"So what's the deal with your partner?" Cerise asks, when she has enough caffeine in her system to talk properly.

Ragnar muses about this for a while. "I'll tell her, of course. We don't keep secrets from each other. I know what she's doing while I'm on the trip and she knows I'm good with that. She knows there's always the possibility I'll end up sleeping with someone when I'm at a convention. Though the idea it happened in a traffic jam might make her raise an eyebrow. She'll probably insist we look at buying a campervan. And next time we go away together, she'll probably insist on bringing her strap-on with her just in case. Not that she goes away without it anyway. There was one time we were in a hotel and she picked up a client in the bar. He wanted her to fuck his ass while I watched. I still don't know how I feel about that, but it paid for the hotel—and the sex afterwards was wonderful." He pauses. "So what are you going to do? And you do have stories like that?"

"Of course I'll tell my partner. Like you, we don't keep secrets." But she's not really sure she means that yet. This out-of-time and out-of-reality experience might not qualify as something she needs to tell. "As for what my partner will do about it ..." She smiled gently. "Probably not as much as I'd hope."

"And what would you hope for?"

"Well, we've both been under a lot of pressure. So we need something that reconnects us. Tight bondage, and a really long session—a whole weekend, maybe, just being a fucktoy and a paintoy, whatever he wants to do with me. And going through all the 'Yes, sir' and 'Thank you for the spanking, master' rituals again." She sighs. "We haven't done that for a loooong time."

They seem to have played themselves out, though. Cerise puts her head against Ragnar's shoulder and sinks into satisfied sleep. Before she finally drifts away, she murmurs "Thank you for fucking me, sir".

Light wakes her. The first streaks of dawn and a sky the color of dirty tin. Ragnar's not there. She shivers and wonders where she is. Oh yeah—between here and there, in a traffic jam. A quick glance out of the window reveals the jam is still there. She finds, then struggles into, her shirt and fleece. The shirt's long enough to cover her thighs, like a short summer dress.

The rear door of the camper opens, bringing a gust of damp air. Cerise wrinkles her nose, not because of the draft but because she has the realization that the back of her van smells like sex.

Ragnar climbs aboard. "The buzz is, everything's mended or made safe or whatever they needed to do to it. We should be on our way shortly."

Cerise nods, understanding that the experience of the night is now over.

"Oh, one other thing," he continues smugly. "You remember I used the Love Gun to zap the couple in the red hatchback? The truck driver told me they were fucking on the hood of their car in the middle of the night." He gives her a twisted smile. "Young couple, of course. They'd probably fuck on the hood of their car in a traffic jam anyway. So was it just coincidence?"

Cerise doesn't have an opinion.

He picks up the Love Gun. "I'll just put this back in my car. But while we're waiting to move, how about another cup of your very wonderful coffee?"

The first sign of action is a police car escorting a heavy crane and an excavator in the opposite lane. By then Ragnar's back in his car ahead of her and they're waiting expectantly. They'd hugged but not kissed, not more than a peck on the cheek anyway. He didn't give her a phone number or an email address. She didn't offer hers. There's a mutual understanding that this was a random and other-reality encounter, never to be repeated.

It takes a few more minutes for them all to get going,

slowly at first, and she follows Ragnar for the next few miles, through a long section of emergency roadwork and under a bridge now supported with much scaffolding. There are more signs to Mountweazel, and he turns in that direction. He waves as he disappears into the distance.

Cerise gets off the interstate forty miles later, where her phone's satnav tells her it intersects with the road that will take her home. But the van still smells of sex, she's just wearing her shirt and fleece, and there are used condoms and bondage tape somewhere in the back. She stops at a service station. Doesn't use any of the facilities apart from a litter bin, to remove evidence of sex. Then she stashes the nipple clamps and bondage tape and lube back in the locker, washes up the mugs and puts her panties and jeans back on.

And she discovers Ragnar's hat with its brass goggles.

For the rest of the trip, she wrestles with the question of whether to tell her partner. She normally wouldn't have any hesitation in doing so, and there's no reason why she shouldn't tell him. But the whole experience was so out-of-place and out-of-time, in a bubble that isn't part of her real world, that it would be like sharing something as ephemeral as a dream. Except she can still taste Ragnar. Still feel his cock in her and the way his ampallang stimulated her. Still feel the after-effects of the clamps. Her muscles retain the exhaustion, the sweaty glory and wicked accomplishment of the sex. And those things are all very un-dreamlike. Plus, every bump and crack in the road feels like a tiny aftershock of sex.

As for the Love Gun—Cerise knows of no technology that would actually work the way the gun did. So it must have just been a symbolic device that allowed her subconscious desires to surface, mustn't it? Except for the couple in the hatchback, who might have fucked on the hood of their car anyway. These thoughts occupy the rest of her journey, but as she turns onto her street she puts those thoughts into the mental space she keeps for unanswerable questions.

Back home, her partner is still at his computer. But he's finished the research project that has occupied all his waking moments for months, and he's obviously prepared for her arrival. There's a smell of cooking in the kitchen and he's vacuumed the house. She strolls in wearing the top hat. "It was left in the van," she explains. "I met a guy in the traffic jam and he forgot to take it with him when we started moving again."

Her partner doesn't seem very curious about the hat, though he asks her about the trip.

"I was on the I38, and everything ground to a halt. A landslide in the section where it cuts through some hills. We were stuck for hours—most of the night, in fact."

"Are you sure?"

"About?" She puts in her injured-innocence face.

"About the route number. I caught something about that on the news last night. Or thought I did. But then I checked Google Maps to see where it was, and it turns out there is no I38. The number's never been used."

Cerise shrugs. "All I can say is we were stopped near

someplace called Mountweazel."

Her partner raises one eyebrow. "*Mountweazel?* You know what a Mountweazel is, right?"

Oh yeah. Of course. The *New Columbia Encyclopedia*, in 1975, had a biographical entry for Lillian Virginia Mountweazel (1942 – 73). She'd been a famous female photographer who died in a fire while working on a commission for *Combustibles* magazine. Except feminists who wanted to celebrate the life of this extraordinary female photographer found out pretty quickly she'd never existed. The entry was fictitious, designed to trap anyone infringing the encyclopedia's copyright. After that, a "Mountweazel" became a generic name for a ghost or fake name in a book or on a map that was put there as a trap to prove theft of intellectual property.

Her partner knows that she knows this, because she told him about it way back when they both worked for a publishing company. It was how they got together in the first place—a shared liking for that kind of obscure knowledge.

No wonder she'd had a weird feeling about the name when she first saw it, signposted on the I38 that she couldn't have driven along because it apparently doesn't exist.

Cerise shrugs. "I dunno. Maybe it's a version of Agloe. You remember, the fictitious place in New York that was put on a map and then people started building houses there because the map said it existed?"

But Cerise has no intention of checking her facts. If the I38 didn't exist and the town of Mountweazel is fictional, her encounter on the road might be a fantasy as well. Except she does have the muscle-memory of her body and a top hat to confirm it ...

She finds and wears her red cloak around the house, nothing but stockings underneath it, liking the sensation of being prey for a rapacious beat. It takes her partner a day to recover his rapacious beast persona, but then she spends the whole weekend in tight bondage, being a fucktoy and a paintoy, for the first time in a very long time. Reconnection is established, equilibrium is restored.

And what happened on the I38 near Mountweazel stays there, an experience a couple of dimensions removed from reality with only a top hat and brass goggles stashed under the bed to prove it ever happened.

GOING UP

LILY HARLEM

G o i n g U p

"Henry, where are we going?" I asked, touching the strip of black velvet he'd used to blindfold me twenty minutes earlier. "Please tell me."

"You'll just have to wait and see," he said, his lips moving against the material at my ear.

His warm breath seeped through to my skin and as always a shudder of delight at his nearness tickled over my body.

"I've told you already, patience is a virtue," he whispered.

"But I wanted to stay in bed," I moaned, thinking of how much I'd enjoyed being naked beneath the duvet in our quaint Oxfordshire hotel room. We hadn't made nearly enough use of our antique bed posts. I still had a few more fantasies I'd like to realize with those, one of which involved tying him up with his silk tie and leather belt and seeing just how much *he* liked being teased.

"It will be worth it, darling," he said softly. "I promise."

The taxi took a sharp bend and I bunched against him. Quickly he wrapped his arm around my shoulders and held me secure. I was glad of his extra support to stop me from sliding on the cool leather seat. My skirt was short and silky and gave no friction. It was a little unnerving to be driven with no sense of the approaching twists and turns in the rural road.

"I thought we were going for a walk and pub lunch today," I said. "When we eventually got up."

"I had a *much* better idea."

I could well imagine the wicked glint that would have been in his eyes as he spoke. Henry Worthington-Foster's ideas were always of the dirty, sexy variety. We'd been dating for six months, an intense whirlwind of wild nights and wilder weekends with no expense spared. He was different to my previous boyfriends. I thought of sex a lot, all the time in fact, and I'd always suspected my libido was higher than average. It had put other men off, but not Henry. Henry kept up with me on all-night-marathon sex sessions and his anything-goes-as-long-as-it-feels-good attitude matched mine.

I tapped my fingers up his leg to his groin then rested my palm over the zipper on his jeans. Beneath the fabric I could feel his fleshy half-mast, happy and expectant but not quite rampant—yet.

"Am I going to get off, where you're taking me?" I asked quietly.

"Get off as in 'be fucked senseless'?" he said loudly.

I giggled. I could just imagine the taxi driver's face. Henry's quintessentially English pronunciation, his rounded vowels and consonants that could cut glass, always pricked people's ears when he'd talk dirty. It didn't fit his tall, eloquent style, floppy dark hair and beautifully tailored country casual outfits.

To me the whole package of Henry was seriously seductive and I was starting to wonder what would happen if he stopped calling to arrange rampant liaisons.

"Why are you laughing?" he asked, shifting his hips and pressing his groin against the palm of my hand a little more. He was always greedy for my touch.

"I guess even my imagination can't begin to think of what you have in store for me this sunny spring morning."

"Let's just say I was listening when you revealed your fantasies last week. You enjoyed the four-poster bed last night, didn't you?"

"Well yes, of course …" My memory whirred. What had I told him? Fuck, it could have been any number of things. The previous week he'd tortured me, sensually of course—with a dildo and a vibrator hovering on insertion into both of my holes—until I'd told him my darkest desires. I'd blurted out a whole host of dirty deeds that I thought might persuade him to complete what he'd started and finish me off.

But it wasn't until he was sure I'd revealed all that he set about hitting my hot spots and rewarding me for my wild confessions.

"Don't look so worried," he said soothingly. "Perhaps I've just chilled a bottle of Taittinger for you to sip as you look out over the vale."

"Mmm, that was on my fantasy list." But by far the tamest of my revelations. I'd always wanted to try the expensive champagne but never had the chance. Sipping it at breakfast time seemed even more decadent.

"Exactly," he said.

"But lots of other things were on that list and—"

He laughed. "Oh, Faye, you're so cute when you're nervous."

"I'm not nervous." I stroked his cock, exploring the length and width of him through his clothing. "I'm just curious."

There was a soft, sweet pressure on my lips as he kissed me. Henry loved to kiss, which was just as well as he had a very sensual mouth. His lips were a little on the thin side and perhaps a bit wide for his face. But like most things about him, his nuances and imperfections made him all the more appealing (not to mention outrageously hot) to me. Faye Jones from Stratford had grabbed herself an aristocrat, who'd have thought it?

Henry was multi-layered. Sure he'd been privately educated, was old-money rich and had all the right connections to catapult him up the career ladder. But there was so much more and I loved peeling back those layers, sampling the delights he had to offer and lapping up the secrets that spilled from his body in the dark of the night.

Loving it to a point where I was falling *in* love with him.

Not that I'd dare tell him that. It might ruin everything.

"Ah, we're almost here," he said, catching my wrist and removing my hand from his groin. "So you'd better stop that. I need to be able to walk across a field."

"A field?" Now that he'd mentioned the champagne I was wondering if he'd organized a breakfast picnic somewhere in the rolling countryside. "A field that leads to where?"

"Must it lead anywhere?"

"It has to lead somewhere ..."

The taxi came to a halt and Henry released my seatbelt.

"Too many questions," he said, opening the car door. "Just wait."

The sweet scent of meadow flowers filtered towards me as did the sound of chirping birds.

"Here," Henry said. "Keep the change."

"Thank you, sir," the taxi driver replied.

"Come on, darling. Time to get out."

"Can I take the blindfold off?"

"In a minute." He tugged me out of the car and my feet, in their flat pumps, settled in long grass that tickled my ankles and shins. It was early, but the welcome warmth of the sun spread over my shoulders. We'd been enjoying a mini heat wave and it seemed set to continue today.

The car door shut and the taxi purred into the distance.

Henry stood behind me, wrapped his arms around my waist and settled my back against his chest. I could feel the outline of his cock nestled against my buttcheeks and his hard forearms felt solid against my belly.

"I didn't want you to see it from a distance," he said. "I wanted you to see this stage of the fantasy in all of its glory."

"Okay ..." I clutched his forearms and rubbed my fingers across the coating of dark hairs that ran over his wrists. Anticipation rippled through me and my heart beat faster. "Show me now and stop teasing me. It's not fair."

He chuckled, shifting me within his embrace. "Here goes."

Releasing his hold, he fiddled with the knot at my nape and the blindfold loosened. Suddenly it slipped downward and I blinked as the bright light of the day attacked my retinas.

Squinting, I looked around. We were indeed in the countryside. Green, rolling hills undulated on the horizon and a copse of silver birches stood to our right. On the other side of the field was a hot-air balloon. It was inflated, its diamond pattern brightly colored—red, green, blue, orange and yellow—with the words *Flights of Fantasy* emblazoned upon it in black lettering.

"Wow," I said, shielding my eyes from the sun.

"I hope you're up for it," Henry said, sliding a reassuring arm around my shoulders and urging me forwards.

"Yes, it's something I've always wanted to do."

"I know. You informed me of that, remember?" He pressed a kiss to my temple.

"Yes, just about."

He smiled. "Come on, Felix is waiting for us."

"Felix?"

"The pilot, Felix Montague, he's an old friend of mine, our fathers were at Eton together."

We marched through the long grass. Several butterflies fluttered out of our way and I paused to navigate around a patch of stinging nettles.

As we approached the balloon it was evident the ropes holding the basket were straining to keep it on the ground. The sound of the flame roared and the man, Felix, who operated the burner turned and waved enthusiastically.

He was tall and lean, much like Henry, but his hair was short and blonde. He wore a pale blue shirt with a navy blue sweater draped over his shoulders. The arms of the sweater were knotted at his sternum.

"So, the balloon ride is the first of the things on your wish list that will be met this morning," Henry said. "I hope you'll enjoy them all."

"I'm sure I will. And, wow, it's the perfect morning for a trip into the sky." I was bubbling with excitement at the thought of soaring through the air. It really was something I'd always wanted to experience.

"Oh, it'll be a perfect morning all right," he said, and that glint I'd come to love flickered in his eyes once again. "Hey, Felix, how are you, old chap?"

"All set," Felix said, smiling our way. He dropped his gaze over me, lingering on the hemline of my ridiculously short khaki skirt. But it wasn't lecherous, just appreciative and I didn't mind. He was cute as a button and I had great legs.

"Let me introduce Faye Jones," Henry said, releasing me and gripping Felix's outstretched hand.

Felix shook hands with Henry and then held his hand out to me.

I placed my fingers within his palm, expecting a shake, but instead he drew my knuckles to his mouth and placed a soft kiss upon them.

"Enchanted," he said, lifting his head but not releasing my hand. "I've heard all about you, Faye but nothing could have prepared me for how beautiful you are."

I laughed. "Aren't you the smooth talker."

He smiled and, judging from the crease lines around his eyes, I guessed that was something he did a lot. "Yeah, that's me. Now come on, climb on board. It's time to go."

Henry stooped and hoisted me into the air. He leaned over the side of the basket and it creaked as he placed me within the whicker walls.

I was surprised by how big it seemed and how high the flame and gas tanks were. There were a few dials and switches too. Looking further up, I was fascinated by the sheer size of the balloon and the apparent nothingness that was keeping it bulbous above me.

"What do you think?" Felix asked.

"I think it's amazing," I said, still looking upwards.

"Well if you like it now, just wait until we're flying high," he said.

Henry jumped into the basket next to me and shoved a hand through his mussed up hair. I wasn't sure if he'd brushed his wayward locks before we'd left the hotel, not that it bothered me. I liked his bed-head look.

He slapped Felix on the back. "Thank for this, I owe you."

Felix laughed. "I owed you, that's why I'm here." He turned to me. "But it's not exactly a hardship. I love flying the balloon and with such pretty company, I'm sure we're going to have an amazing time."

"We are indeed." Henry bent double and flicked the lid on a hamper that was the same chestnut-brown as the walls and floor surrounding me. "Hold these, Faye."

He passed me two crystal flutes, then after the rattle of ice sliding in metal, he produced a bottle of Taittinger.

"Oh, you didn't?" I exclaimed.

"Of course I did. I want this to be a perfect fantasy flight for you," he said, grinning and wiping drops from the bottle with a red-checkered cloth.

"It's very sweet of you," I said.

"I'm a sweet guy." He twitched his eyebrows suggestively.

"Ha, is that what he's been telling you, Faye?" Felix said, lugging a sandbag into the basket. "That he's sweet."

"I guess sweet isn't really the first word that comes to

mind," I said, watching Henry expertly unwrap the foil from the cork. "But it's certainly up near the top." Along with sexy, handsome, thoughtful, sinfully dirty …

"I'm glad you think I'm sweet," Henry said, firing the cork into the air. Instantly a glug of froth overspilled the mouth of the bottle and I quickly held out the glasses to catch it.

"Hey don't make a mess," Felix said, frowning.

"Ah, don't fret," Henry said, skilfully filling both flutes and not spilling a drop. He set the champagne back on ice and then clinked his glass with mine.

"Bottoms up," he said, licking his lips.

"My favorite position," I said with a grin.

"Glad to hear it," Felix said with a laugh then reached for a walkie-talkie hanging on a length of cord. "This is FF. Do you read, FM?" he said into it.

"Loud and clear," came a crackly reply.

"We're ready for take off," Felix said.

"Roger."

"Who's that?" I asked.

"The chase crew, I needed to have some support on the ground to get this baby ready," he said. "But watch it now. Hold on."

Suddenly we lurched to the right and then upward. Henry gripped both me and the rim of the basket.

I grabbed his arm and balanced my drink over the side in case any liquid should spill.

"We're off," Felix said, reaching to the middle of the

basket and pulling on a lever. The hiss of the increased flame filled my ears and the heat of it simmered on to my cheeks.

My guts rolled in excitement as I swigged champagne, barely noticing the deliciously dry bubbles popping on my tongue.

Henry pressed a kiss to my cheek. "Are you all right?"

"Yes, yes, never better. This is great."

"Oh my darling. It's going to get so much more exciting in a few minutes."

"Really?" I asked. "Why, what else do you have in store for me?" I gestured around. "What could be better than this?"

He winked, an infuriating habit of his when he wasn't going to tell me something, and sipped on his drink. "Mmm, good stuff," he said, studying the golden liquid. "Really good stuff."

"Say goodbye to terra firma," Felix called excitedly.

I spun and looked over the side. We were already about twenty feet into the air. The dotty meadow flowers were blurring into a mass of color and the flattened patch of grass from beneath the basket was getting smaller by the second.

"Where are we going?" I asked.

"Up," Henry said. "We're going up of course."

I laughed and turned within his arms.

"Do you like the bubbly?" he asked.

"It's lovely." I drained my glass.

He set it, along with his, in the hamper basket.

"This baby flies beautifully," Felix said, checking a dial that looked like a compass. "I've been flying her for over a year now and she just gets better."

Again I looked up. The air was hazy, the heat distorting the black lines that outlined the diamond shaped pattern.

Henry pushed my hair over my ears and cupped my cheeks, tipped my face to his. "I'm glad you're wearing that disgracefully short skirt," he whispered against my lips.

"Why?"

"Because I'm going to need easy access."

I wriggled against him. His cock was noticeably harder than it had been before. "We can't … what about Felix?"

"Like I said, Felix and I go back a long way."

The wind caught the balloon and we shifted to the left. I hung onto Henry even more tightly.

"Air current's perfect," Felix said, shielding his eyes and looking into the distance. "This should take us on a nice long ride, it couldn't be better conditions."

"Go with it, Faye," Henry said quietly. "Just go with it and I promise it will be everything you hoped for."

He kissed me, and even though I was full of questions I melted into him. He backed me against the wall of the basket, which hit below my shoulders, and began a slow, sensual dance with his tongue.

He tasted of champagne, of mint and of Henry—a unique blend of flavors that always got me burning up for him, no matter where we were.

The alcohol hit my brain, not much, just a little, adding to the wonderful floaty feeling I already had. I felt light, high, my body was buzzing not least because Henry was running his hands over my body. His hands encircled my waist before gliding down to my hips. My skirt only traveled a few inches down my thighs and soon he was stroking my bare flesh.

I shivered a little, in anticipation, not cold, and ran my fingers into his hair. The thick curls knotted around my knuckles and he groaned as I pulled them, the way he had last night when he'd been going down on me and I'd yanked on his hair when the sensations overwhelmed me.

My pussy clenched. The mere memory of that blisteringly intense orgasm was turning me on and, combined with the way he was kissing and stroking me, pure lust was now coursing through my veins.

His touch snuck beneath my skirt and his fingers skimmed over my pussy lips, teasing the ridges of flesh through my sheer underwear.

"Henry," I gasped into his mouth. The need for more was instant but uncertainty held me back.

"Shh," he murmured. "Remember you said you wanted to have sex in front of an audience?"

"I did?" Probably. I'd said lots of things that night.

He chuckled. "Yes, fantasy number twenty-two if I remember correctly, though you were getting pretty desperate by that point."

He nudged my thighs apart with his knee.

"Let me touch you, here, now," he whispered, again rubbing my pussy lips through the material of my panties. "Let me make you come as we're going up … and with Felix watching."

A quiver of arousal shot through me, engorging my clit and making me grind against his fingers.

Damn he's so persuasive.

I looked over his shoulder.

Felix was staring at us. A half-smirk tugged at the corner of his lips and his pupils were wide; clearly he had a touch of voyeur in him.

"Don't mind me," he said. "Henry's been quite specific about how this morning is going to fulfill your fantasies, and I think you're going to enjoy it just fine." He paused. "Hell, I know I am."

He leaned back against the basket and crossed one leg over the other. At the apex of his pale cream chinos, a heavy bulge seemed to stretch the fabric.

"Darling, relax," Henry said against my ear. "Relax as I touch you. Felix is hardly a simpering virgin. He'll adore seeing you come, you're glorious when you just let go."

Oh, what the hell.

I'd never been described as shy and I was in a basket with two seriously gorgeous guys. What harm could a quick little orgasm do when I was feeling this turned on? And Henry was right, it *did* turn me on, the thought of us being watched. Of *me* being watched. "Okay," I said quickly, before

I changed my mind.

"Good girl." He slipped his fingers past the flimsy fabric between my legs and through the wetness that had gathered there. He knew my body so well and within seconds he was easing two fingers into me.

My eyes fluttered shut and I squeezed my internal muscles.

"Always so warm and wet for me," he said then kissed me again, thoroughly, hungrily. His breath was fast and ragged, his chest solid as he pressed into me. He was excited by this too and that turned me on all the more.

I clung to his shoulders, aware of Felix releasing more hot air into the balloon, and kissed Henry back with an urgency for more.

He moaned into my mouth and caught my clit with the heel of his hand.

My heart rate rocketed, my pulse thudding in my ears. Damn, if I'd thought I'd start the day off in bed with a languid climax I'd been very wrong. This one was building fast and furious. Henry was slipping his fingers in and out of me like a stubby cock and his palm rubbed wickedly at my needy nub.

"Ahhh … ah …" I panted after a few minutes and breaking our kiss. "That's it, don't stop …"

"I won't … fuck you're beautiful."

I glanced at Felix. He was only a few feet away. His mouth was slack and he was rubbing his clean-shaven chin. The searing glint in his eye told me he was enjoying my performance.

Henry altered his style just slightly, speeding the pumping action of his fingers and mashing into my clit with renewed vigor. The man certainly knew where all my sweet-spots were.

"I'm ... I'm coming ..." I gasped, throwing my head back and staring at the inside of the balloon. We shifted to the left and Henry tightened his hold on me to keep me secure between him and the edge of the basket.

Relieved that he had me, I let myself topple into my orgasm. The colors above me became psychedelic, fuzzing and swaying. My pelvis released and then thumped through my climax. Juicy noises squelched from me as Henry siphoned out my pleasure to the very end.

"Yes, oh, yes, fuck ..." I gasped, "Never thought ... I'd ... on a balloon."

Henry used his free hand to cradle the back of my head. He drew my face to his.

"I've got you," he said. "I've got you." He slowed his movements and the near violent spasms in my cunt eased.

"Yes, yes ..." I managed, panting.

Henry smiled then looked over his shoulder at Felix. "Enjoy that?" he asked.

"Fuck, you know damn well I did."

Felix stepped up to Henry and wrapped his fingers around his right bicep. He tugged until Henry pulled from my pussy and held his hand up between the three of us.

Silvery moisture sparkled on his middle two fingers

and the aroma of my sex swirled in the air.

Felix leaned forwards, poked out his tongue and swept it over Henry's fingers.

Henry laughed. "Just remember, no matter how much you like the taste, she's mine."

"Of course," Felix said, frowning and then looking at me. "I get that, but damn, she fucking delicious."

"Just as well I'm up for sharing today," Henry said, pulling his arm from Felix's grip and then turning to me. "Sharing my woman because I know it's something she wants … no, make that *needs* to do."

I simply stared, first at Henry and then at Felix. Two tall, posh guys who oozed the sex-appeal of the truly confident. How lucky was I? And it seemed, right now, I was being given the chance to have them both. At the same time.

I want a threesome I'd yelled that night of fantasy revelations. Why? Henry has asked. *Because I want to be adored by two men, penetrated by two men, fucked senseless by two men.* Is that your deepest, darkest fantasy? *Yes, yes, yes.*

He had a good memory, my Henry; and it seemed he also a good friend who was willing to help out.

"Let me see your cock," I said to Felix.

There was a moment of stunned silence. Like that had been the last thing either of them had expected me to say. Then Henry laughed, stroking my cheek with the back of his hand. "Never too shy to speak your mind, are you!" he said.

I smiled, in what I hoped was a sultry, sexy manner.

"I just want to check out the goods before I agree to this," I told them with feigned innocence.

"Oh, I'm sure you'll find the goods most agreeable," Felix said. He was already unbuckling his shiny brown belt. "I have no doubt about that."

The adrenaline thrill of our mile-high ménage threatened to overwhelm me, and I took a moment to calm myself. On the horizon, the distant hills looked like big, soft pillows as we drifted slowly and silently along, the treetops, village homes and dreamy church spires of Oxfordshire far below us. If I hadn't been so excited about what was about to happen, I would have paused to admire the vista.

As it was, Felix had lowered his chinos, and the pair of black Armani boxers bunched within them, to his knees. His grateful erection bounced happily out from its confines.

I licked my lips. He had a neat, circumcised cock. The shaft was a deep burgundy with twisting veins and the glans a shiny plum-color. His slit was dark and deep and his balls, sprinkled with hair the same straw shade as on his head, hung heavy beneath.

"Will this do for Madam's fantasy?" he asked, grinning and wrapping his fist around the length.

"Very nicely," I said, then raised an eyebrow to Henry. "But that's only one."

Henry grinned. "Your wish is my command."

He toed off his deck shoes, shucked off his jeans and underwear to stand in nothing but his polo shirt. His penis jutted out proud and upright, with the hem of his shirt skimming the root.

This was absolutely exhilarating. "Let's lose all the clothes," I said. "My threesome fantasy involves flesh-on-flesh. *Lots* of flesh-on-flesh."

As Henry peeled off his top and Felix quickly shed his clothes, I wriggled out of my t-shirt, skirt and underwear.

The cool morning breeze on my naked skin was erotic in itself. The sharpness of the wicker behind me and the dampness between my legs all reminded me of how surreal this moment was. But it was real—real and incredibly sexy.

"This thing okay for a few minutes?" Henry asked, nodding upwards.

"Yep, she's nice and steady," Felix answered.

"Great," I said, "That means you won't have to think about it while I do this ..." I dropped to my knees and took a cock in each hand.

"Yesss ... baby," Felix said, resting his hand on my head and gulping in a breath. "Go for it."

"Fuck," Henry gasped, as I squeezed his cock. "You're so fucking sexy and eager all the damn time."

"It's how you make me feel," I said, gazing up at him. I adored it when he had that gooey expression on his face. It made me believe that I held his heart—just for a moment—as well as his dick. It was the way he looked at me, like I was the center of his universe and nothing else existed.

I leaned forwards and swiped my tongue over the tip of his cock. He was hot and hard and the glossy groove tasted slightly salty.

Then I turned my attention to Felix and repeated the action.

"Mmm …" he moaned, "But I want more."

I opened my mouth, wide, and took him deep. His glans grazed across my palate and his shaft sat heavy on my tongue. As I took him further and further into my throat, I pumped Henry's shaft, just the way he liked it, firm with a bit of a twist when I reached the base.

Felix tightened his grip on my hair.

My scalp tingled.

I withdrew, bobbed back down and breathed in his musky, woody scent. He was different to Henry who used a citrusy showergel and the fruity smell lingered. But I liked Felix's aroma, it turned me on, flooded my senses. I beat down my gag-reflex, something I'd become pretty adept at, and attempted to bury my nose in his short pubic hair.

"Fuck, she can deep-throat," he groaned above me.

"Like a pro," Henry said, pride in his voice. "Fucking amazing, isn't it?"

"Oh god … yes."

Felix shifted towards me and his cock twitched in my mouth. I had him so far down now, nestled on the very base of my tongue. I created a gentle suction, pulling on the delicate skin on his glans.

"Fuck," he groaned above me. "That's going to make me come."

"Faye, darling, go easy on him. He's not as used to your skills as I am," Henry said, touching my shoulder.

I slowly withdrew, my lips caressing Felix's cock and sliding over all the bulging veins on his shaft as I pulled back.

I caught his erection in my palm and looked up at him. His cheeks were flushed and his pupils wide.

I smiled.

He blew out a breath that tickled over my face.

Turning my attention to Henry, I saw that anticipation had reddened his cheeks. He knew exactly what he was in for and just how fast I could push him to the point of no control. Giving blowjobs was something of a specialty of mine, or so he'd led me to believe of late.

"You ready?" I asked.

He nodded, slowly, a knowing smile playing at his lips.

I shifted my knees on the hard whicker, then slid his beautiful dick into my mouth. As before, I caressed the cock in my hand, Felix's, at the same time and was rewarded with a double groan of pleasure from above.

"Wait, hang on a sec," Felix suddenly said, stepping away and out of my grip.

With Henry's cock bloating my cheeks, I glanced at Felix. He checked a dial, scanned the horizon and then blasted the flame once more.

"We need to go up a few hundred feet to stay with the current," he said.

Of course I couldn't answer, but I was glad he still was in some kind of command of our skyward journey. I didn't want to blow his mind, just his dick.

"Ah, yes ... fuck, baby, you look amazing," Henry said, stroking my fat cheeks.

His words were an aphrodisiac and my body hummed with pleasure. I was already wet between my legs from my orgasm, but I was dampening further and my nipples were tight little beads.

I increased the speed, creating a rhythmic in-out motion, taking Henry right to the back of my throat each time. It only took a few strokes before the taste of pre-cum began leaking into my mouth.

"Jesus, that's it ... give me a break ..." he gasped, pulling back.

He fell from my mouth, but instantly Felix was there, his erection in his palm. Without a word he fed his cock between my waiting lips.

I took it happily, slurping and sucking as the smooth domed head of his glans slid in deep.

"Ahh ... yeah ..." he said softly, placing his hands in my hair. He took control of my movements, pumping his hips and holding my head steady. I let him thrust in as deep as he wanted. My throat a yielding cavern for him to fuck.

"So damn good ..." he gasped. "Jesus ..."

His cock was rigid and becoming more so by the second. When he withdrew, I quickly laved at the end before he sank deep again. But this time, it wasn't just his cock sinking, he also sank to his knees in front of me.

"I can't stand up for this ... it's too much ..." he said.

I stayed with him, my head now buried in his groin

and my ass thrust up into the air.

I was aware of Henry's hands as he squeezed in behind me and parted my legs. The breeze instantly cooled the dampness between my thighs.

Henry's fingers were quick and deft, spreading the slick moisture over my folds and circling my clit.

I moaned around Felix's penis. My pussy was begging for attention, clenching lewdly in anticipation of Henry touching me there.

"I'm going to fuck you, Faye," Henry said, his free hand gripping me firmly. "While you suck Felix."

I couldn't answer but I wriggled my hips a little, hoping that would assure him that I approved of his plan.

"Spit-roast I think you called it," Henry said, obliging my needy pussy and slipping two, then three fingers inside me.

I moaned, a muffled, breathy sound.

"Spit-roast was one of your fantasies, wasn't it?" he asked.

I moaned again. *I want a big, fat cock in my mouth and another in my cunt, spit-roast style,* I'd said, *yes, that's a top fantasy.*

"Dirty, horny girl," Felix said. With one hand he stroked my hair, but with the other he'd bunched my hair tight into his fist. "So fucking dirty and horny. Perfect."

I pulled up, released his cock and turned to Henry. "Do it," I panted. "Fucking spit-roast me."

Henry laughed, withdrew his fingers and, as I gobbled Felix back into my mouth, Henry thrust his cock deep inside me.

"Ahhh ..." I managed, the sound vibrating in my chest and around Felix's penis.

Henry's first plunge always brought with it a delicious stretching of my insides. He was long and granite-hard and in this ass-up position he'd shoved right up against my cervix creating a dense, intoxicating pleasure.

He pulled out and plunged back in quickly. His balls squashed into my spread labia as his thrusting forced me deeper onto Felix.

My head was spinning, my body tingling all over. I felt so owned, so possessed by these two aroused, demanding men. There was also a sense of pride that I had them both, at the same time, inside me.

The heat in my pussy was increasing with each stroke from Henry, as was the burning pressure building in my pelvis. Saliva dribbled from my chin as I frantically suckled on Felix. Wild slurping noises spilt from my lips and the sound of my ass bouncing against Henry's abdomen made a steady *slap, slap, slap*.

"God ... that's good ... I'm already so close ..." Henry said, and the tension in his voice told me he meant it.

Felix was leaking pre-cum into my mouth, a steady groan rumbling from deep in his chest. His heat and scent surrounded me as I breathed within the pocket of air at his groin.

Suddenly a sharp, stinging slap rang out on my right buttock.

Henry knew that a slice of pain could sometimes tip me over the edge.

My flesh jiggled as the pain bloomed. I could feel every fingerprint blistering a mark onto my skin.

I squealed first, and then moaned in delight as I harnessed the burn, let it ripple to my clit and then tightened my pussy around Henry's shaft to hold the throb there.

"Get ready for it," Felix gasped, knitting his fingers against my scalp. "Fuck ... I'm coming ..." As he'd spoken, a wave of release pulsed up through his erection, resulting in a wash of semen at the base of my throat.

I swallowed it down, as much as I could.

He pulled out and warm cum dribbled from my mouth. Some of it was guided back in again on his return plunge.

A wave of dizziness hit me along with the final climb to my orgasm. It was there, a deep and satisfying explosion all set for detonation.

I thought of what I must look like, bared on my hands and knees and plugged with stout cock from both ends. The vision toppled me over the edge and I allowed my climax to ravish me.

Henry joined me and as I became a pulsing mass of ecstasy he gushed into my pussy. His dick jerked as each crest of bliss poured from him and coated my insides.

I hugged his pulsing penis with my flexing internal muscles, beautiful spasms of release that had me moaning and groaning around Felix.

This fantasy had been worth revealing on every level.

Felix withdrew from my mouth and toppled backwards onto his backside. The basket shifted a little under his weight.

His member was still erect and shiny, glistening with our shared contributions.

I stared at him, enjoying the last few thuds of my orgasm as I pulled in much needed oxygen.

"Fuck, that was intense," Felix gasped. "You okay?"

"Yeah ... never ... better ..."

Behind me, Henry had slowed and was lazily stroking in and out of me. I was slick with our mutual spendings, and the frictionless motion was like a soothing balm to my ravished internal flesh. I'd have been happy to let him keep doing that until I was ready to climax again. In fact, he had done exactly that on a few bliss-infused occasions.

He rubbed his hand up my spine, to my nape and feathered his fingers through my messy hair. "Did that hit the spot, darling?"

"Yes ... I'm sure you could tell ..." I was still enjoyably breathless and light-headed.

He chuckled. "You should have seen yourself. You looked amazing." His hand stroked back down over my shoulders, now damp with perspiration from all my efforts.

"Tell me. What did I look like?"

"Like a woman who knows what she wants and isn't afraid to take it," he said.

"You looked and felt incredible," Felix added, his

knees flopping outwards as he breathed heavily. His balls hung weightily towards the basket floor and his now softening cock curved like a saber over his thigh. "So beautiful and giving." His mouth twisted into a wicked grin. "I'm certainly glad Henry asked me to help out with these fantasies of yours."

"Me too." I curled my hands into fists as Henry withdrew completely. The basket beneath me had marked my palms where I'd been balancing and I was becoming aware of the dents and creases in my hands and my knees.

"Come here," Henry said, and he wrapped me in the blue tartan blanket that had been resting beside the picnic basket.

I was suddenly glad of the warmth. My damp skin goosepimpling as we floated through the high, cool air.

Felix stood and started fiddling with the gas, releasing another spurt of flames. He was completely at ease with his nudity and his spent, exposed cock; and I admired his body confidence. Not that he shouldn't be confident. He was athletic with a taut, toned musculature. I could imagine him running or cycling or climbing regularly. Taking to the slopes in the winter and manning a yacht in the South of France in the summer.

Henry gathered me onto his lap, so that I was wrapped up warm and cocooned within the huddle of his embrace. A sudden weariness came over me as I rested my head back onto his shoulder.

"Shh," he whispered. "Close your eyes."

"But I don't want to miss the flight?" I said then

stifled a yawn. "The view. I want to see the view from up here."

He laughed. "We've got plenty of time, and besides, you're going to need your strength."

"I am?" I touched his chin and stroked over the small scar he had there—an old polo accident.

"Yes. Five minutes rest, that's an order young lady."

The basket swayed and drifted upwards towards the sun. I shut my eyes, safe in Henry's arms, enjoying the feeling of flying high as I was lulled into a doze.

"Blenheim," Felix said. "We're over Blenheim Palace. Didn't you want to show Faye that?"

"Yes. Darling, wake up," Henry said, giving me a little jostle.

I hadn't really been asleep, just resting in a post climactic glow. But the thought of seeing Blenheim, from above, was just too much to resist and I jolted myself from slumber.

"I'm awake," I said, wriggling within Henry's arms.

He pressed a kiss to my temple then helped me stand, still with the soft woolen blanket around my shoulders. A rivulet of cum trickled down my inner thigh, and I reached for a napkin from within the picnic basket to wipe it away.

"Sorry," he said sheepishly, holding out his hand to take the paper from me.

"I'm not complaining. Condoms were driving me

nuts." I stroked my index fingers down his chest and circled his small dark nipple.

A tremble traveled over his skin.

"I like how close we feel, now that we've gotten rid of the need for them," I whispered.

"Me too, damn it, me too." He licked his lips and then kissed me slow and sensually.

"You two need more bubbly," Felix said, interrupting us. "Here, sip on this and admire the palace."

Still within Henry's embrace, I took a flute of champagne from Felix. Henry took one too and clinked the rim to mine.

I took a sip. "Aren't you having one?" I asked Felix.

"Gosh, no, I'm flying, don't want to lose my pilot's license."

"Ah, I see."

Henry urged me to the side of the basket and pointed downwards. "What do you think?"

I looked over the edge. Beneath us was a huge expanse of green landscape dotted with trees and dominated by an enormous building accessed via a bridge. The bridge spanned a royal-blue lake that shimmered in the morning sunshine. It fed a rod-straight road that ended on the biggest driveway I'd ever seen. It was a golden hue and I couldn't tell if it was gravel or paving. Rising upwards all around it was a sandy-bricked palace with imposing pillars at the entrance and a huge number of ornate chimney stacks sprouting from the roof.

"It's beautiful," I said, before enjoying my champagne again. My mouth was dry and, as I remembered why, I couldn't resist a glance at Felix's cock. He was semi-erect; clearly a few minutes rest had done him good.

He caught me studying his dick and gave me that posh-boy-gone-bad grin that sent a flutter of interest to my groin. Damn, I was even more insatiable than usual today and I wondered if it was the high altitude.

"The gardens are stunning," Henry was saying. "Must take hours of upkeep and they're so symmetrical."

"Yes." I drew my attention back to the view. On either side of the building were two main gardens that looked, from here, like they were highly manicured—large circular beds of bright flowers and neat topiary hedges enclosed in old stone walls. Though really it was hard to see, given how high up we were. The cars in the parking lot looked like toys, and I used their perspective size to give myself an idea of scale.

Yes, Blenheim really was enormous.

I drained my champagne, enjoying the decadence of guzzling something so expensive.

Henry laughed and pointed at a maze set back from the main house. "How would you like to get lost in there with me sometime?"

"Anytime." I passed him my empty glass and then curled my fingers over the stiff edge of the basket. "As long as we can do it naked." I let the blanket slide from my shoulders and crumple to the floor. The freedom of being in the sky, everything quiet and wistful while being completely absent of clothes was wonderfully liberating and completely self-indulgent.

He set our empty glasses aside and kissed the curve of my shoulder. "I'm liking the way you think," he said against my skin, his breath warm and tickly. "Naked anything with you is good."

"Including hot air ballooning," I said, leaning over a little more, so that my breasts squashed against the basket and my hair caught on the breeze.

"Yes, including hot air ballooning."

Felix came to stand on the other side of me so I was sandwiched between them as I stared downward at the lush greenery below.

"You have such a beautiful ass," Felix said, smoothing his hand down my back and over my rump. "Perfect handful."

"I agree," Henry said, also drifting his palm down my spine and then trailing his fingers over the other cheek and down to my thigh.

"You left quite a mark," Felix said, rubbing against the small patch of stinging heat left behind from Henry's thwack at the height of my pleasure.

"Her skin blushes beautifully," Henry told him, "Whether it's a hand or a crop."

I sighed, remembering *that* night of fun.

"I should think a paddle too," Felix said, palming a cheek and squeezing a little.

"Yes, I'm sure," Henry agreed. "Haven't tried that yet though. Must get round to it."

A sensual buzz went through me at being admired so, and being spoken of as though I was an object of sexual perfection. I tipped my head further forwards, allowing my hair to fall over my face and dance in the wind.

Four big hands were stroking over me, caressing the flesh on my back, my ass and my thighs. My pussy twitched with renewed interest and as I stared at a distant meandering river, I had to resist pinching myself to make sure I wasn't dreaming. That this was real and not a fantasy.

The stroking became more inquisitive, kneading here, pinching there, until two different hands separated the fleshy globes of my ass, exposing my cleft and the intimate opening there. With any other men, this could have been too intrusive, but we three had shared so much already that I trusted their exploration.

"Mmm, cute," Felix said.

A finger, I wasn't sure whose, traced down the sensitive skin between my cheeks and then settled over my anus.

I jerked involuntarily, but then forced myself still. The first touch of somewhere so sensitive always elicited that response, but I didn't want them to think that I wanted them to stop.

"Have you two …?" Felix trailed off before he finished the question.

From his words, I guessed it was he who was applying the pressure at the center of my pucker.

"Yes, she loves it," Henry said forthrightly, and then

again kissed the edge of my shoulder. "*I* love it, with her."

"I bet you do."

Felix's finger left that spot, but just for a second, only to return a moment later, cool and slippery. There must have been a stash of lube in the picnic basket. Henry really had thought of everything.

I kept my gaze fixed on the earth far below us, my ass up and my back arched. Anticipation had my heart beating fast and had given my cleavage an excited sheen. My legs felt a little shaky, like I had too much adrenaline coursing through my system, so I locked my knees and tried to stay focused.

I stared at a boat on the winding river. Small and white, it left a frothy trail behind it that fanned out into a 'v' shape.

Someone, Henry I thought, spread me so wide that all of my intimacy must have been in full view. I could only imagine the lewd image I presented. My labia puffy and swollen, moisture no doubt glistening in the well of my entrance, and the taut wrinkles of skin around my rosebud now glossy with lube.

A tremble attacked my belly, tugging at what felt like a thread of arousal from my clit to my navel. I shifted my hips, forwards and back, silently giving permission for entry.

"She wants to do it," Henry said softly.

"Yes," Felix replied, "You're one lucky man, old boy."

"I know. Believe me I know."

"Uh … mmm …" I groaned, widening my eyes and

staring at the boat. Felix had slid into my ass, one long finger. Knuckle deep.

I clenched my sphincter, hugging his digit.

"Damn, so tight," Felix said. "You really get your whole piece in here?"

"Yes, no problem," Henry replied. His soothing hands caressed my shoulders and back, gliding over the goosebumps that had sprung up there. "A bit of gentle stretching and she limbers up beautifully."

I shut my eyes. I knew what was coming.

Another finger.

The widening of my ass increased, the burn within the slick, soft tissues; a blissful heat that made me instantly want more.

Felix wriggled his fingers inside me, stroking my softness.

"Oh, yes, that's it," he said softly. "Much better."

I gritted my teeth and gripped the side of the basket. Henry and I often indulged in anal play but it always took me a few minutes to relax into it.

"That's it, just stay like that for a bit, move your fingers in and out," Henry said. "She'll be just fine."

Henry knew me so well. I enjoyed having him conduct this concert, without a word required from me.

"I want to fuck her here," Felix said, his voice clipped and excited. "Jesus, I really want to, Henry."

"You can. That's what she wants. One stiff cock in her ass and the other in the front." He leaned close to me, drawing my shoulder into his warm chest. "That's right isn't it, Faye? You want two cocks inside you, don't you?"

"Yes ... fuck, yes, please ..." Damn, he knew me so well. He'd been so in tune with the fantasies I'd revealed, picking out the very best, the truest and the most closely treasured dreams.

Henry laughed softly. "Okay, darling, in that case, hang on for the ride."

I was hanging on all right, to the edge of the basket.

Felix withdrew his fingers from my ass and my tight ring of muscle clenched. Instantly I missed having him there and I mewled in complaint. I was so turned on, so ready for this.

"Wait a second," Henry said. "He's got to rubber up."

As he'd spoken, the slight scent of latex drifted past my nose along with the tiniest corner of pink foil from a Durex wrapper. I watched it twist and twirl on the breeze, not really falling, just skipping along hundreds of feet above the earth.

"Faye, relax okay. Any time you want to stop, you just let me know," Felix said, curling his fingers around my hips.

"Mmm ... ah ... ah ..." I panted, although it was unlikely that I'd want to stop any time soon.

The head of his cock felt impossibly wide as he exerted a firm pressure at my entrance.

"Bear down," Henry said, pushing my hair from the side of my face and kissing my brow. "Let him in."

I took a deep breath and pushed those practiced muscles downwards.

Felix took full advantage and eased through the taut ring. On and on he went, prising me open, stretching me around his smooth glans.

I could feel every millimeter of the expansion and then, as he sank deeper, the flare and ridge of his cockhead.

"Jesus ... I'm in," Felix said breathily. "Look at that. What a gorgeous fucking sight."

Henry raised his head to look, though he still held my hair back from my face.

I panted through the exquisite sensation of being so wide, and relished a tug of wicked delight as once again I wondered just what the hell I looked like. What the men were seeing now—Felix's hard flesh penetrating me from behind. The skin shiny and taut around his sheathed cock, lube glistening on the shaft and my pussy damp and rosy with need.

"Yes, that's it. Now go deep. All the way," Henry said. "Then I can go in too."

Felix groaned long and loud, sliding steadily deeper and deeper inside me.

I curled my toes on the basket floor and focused on long, straight tractor tracks in a field. The density of the sensation in my ass was robbing my ability to think. Felix had a stout, chunky cudgel of a penis, and he was filling me to the max.

"That's it ... I'm in," he sighed.

I could feel his balls touching the lips of my pussy and his stomach pressing against my ass. He was as deep as he could possibly go and damn it felt so good.

"My turn," Henry said. "Turn to me."

What? I had to move, with a cock buried to the hilt in my ass?

I was about to protest but Felix locked his arms around my waist and pulled me straight, so that my back was pressed against his chest.

"Oh, god … really?" I managed. The shift in position had widened my already stretched aperture even more. The very root of Felix's cock pushing into me at its thickest girth.

I shut my eyes and gripped Felix's forearms. They were tense and the tendons roped beneath the skin.

He took a step backwards and I was forced onto my tiptoes. Impaled upon him, I could do nothing but follow.

"Here," he said. "Reach behind me, hold on."

He'd moved into the corner of the basket and, with Felix supporting me, I rested my hands on the two sides of the basket to give me better leverage upon the shaft currently buried inside me.

"Darling, you look glorious," Henry said. "Here, drink."

I opened my eyes. Henry was standing in front of me holding a full glass of Taittinger. The bubbles frothed and fizzed over the rim.

I parted my lips and he fed me the fizzing liquid. I gulped greedily. Wanting more, more of everything. Some champagne spilt onto my breasts, slipping and sliding over my nipples.

Henry spotted this and stooped to lick a dribble before it reached Felix's arm.

I groaned and my pussy clenched, feeling unbearably empty while elsewhere I was so full. My fantasy was to have two dicks, and I wanted Henry inside me too. I wasn't sure if it was a physical possibility for me, but I was willing to try. I'd managed a dildo and a vibrator before, but this was different. This was real.

"Henry, wait," Felix said. "We need more gas. The lever on the right, pull it clockwise."

"Absolutely."

Henry turned, fiddled with the gas canisters and the now familiar roar of the flame blasted around us. I glanced upwards to see the bright orange burst of energy and the sides of the balloon ripple with the heat.

"I'm sure I'd lose my license for this," Felix muttered. "But fuck, it's worth it."

Henry spun back to me, his cock in his fist.

"You ready for me?" he asked.

I nodded. "Yes," I gasped. "Yes … now."

He grinned, a real indulgent and sinful smile that made all my nerve endings throb. Fuck, this man was all I'd ever dreamed of and more.

I stared into his pale blue eyes, such a contrast to his dark hair and golden skin. His lashes were thick and black making the blueness of his irises all the more startling.

"Henry," I said. "I …"

He touched his lips to mine. "Shh, just enjoy. This is all for you." He stooped and threaded his right arm beneath my left leg. He then drew his arm upwards, so that my leg was draped over it, and I presented an even more vulnerable display than I had before.

I moaned as my hip complained but it soon turned into a groan of pleasure when he plunged two fingers into my front.

Felix let out a grunt that blew hot against my ear and vibrated into my back.

"Henry," I gasped.

"You'll be able to take us both," he said. "Just let the tension go."

"Easy for you to say," Felix said, "Damn it's great like this. Fuck, Faye you're amazing."

I reached for Henry with my free hand and slid it around the back of his neck as he lifted my other leg and supported me completely. I watched as he bent his knees and fed his cock into me.

Felix was taking up a lot of room, and Henry struggled to get the bulbous tip in. But after a little readjustment and a little push, he was there.

"That's it," I gasped, hoping with everything that I had that I'd be able to accommodate them both.

"Yes," Henry hissed, his breath smelling of sweet champagne. "Yes, fuck, yes." He drove upwards, filling me, sliding his cock in next to Felix's, with only a thin partition separating their hot, hard shafts.

I cried out, pleasure flirting with pain as he filled all the remaining space that I had. His pubic bone came into contact with my clit and he ground against it, just the way he knew I liked.

I felt my eyes roll back in my head and my breaths came to a stop. The sensation of having my clit spark to life while being so full was like nothing I'd felt before.

"Breathe," Henry said against my lips. "You have to breathe darling or all of this will stop."

I sucked in a lungful of air and focused on his handsome face. The wind ruffled his hair and a curl, shaped like a comma, was tapping against the lashes on his right eye. His cheeks were flushed to a pale rose.

"Yes," I said, "I'll breathe."

"Good girl."

I felt as hot and full as the balloon above me, pleasure blasting up through me from between my legs right to the top of my head, as fierce and as unrelenting as the gas jets on full blast.

"It's too good," Henry said, "But I ... I've got to make it last ... just a little ..." His eyes locked on mine, and he gritted his teeth with the effort of staving off his orgasm. He thrust up against me, again kneading my clit with his body.

Wetness gushed from me, I was close too. Being so full of these men had me near the edge, and with Henry rolling against me, my orgasm wouldn't take much stoking.

Felix's breath was ragged in my ear, and I felt myself floating into an oblivion that seemed even higher than the balloon.

"Yes, my darling," Henry said. "Come for me, we'll hold you, keep you together. It's going to be intense, okay."

"Yes." As I'd spoken a small sob erupted from me. I wanted to come, but it was going to be an enormous climax. My pussy and my ass were going to pulsate so hard around two big cocks. I worried briefly at the toll such extreme pleasure could take upon my little body.

"Take me with you," Henry said, his lips moving against my cheek. "Come and I'll come too, you've got me on the edge."

I couldn't hold back. His wickedly skilled movements had my clit screaming for release. And I let go.

"Ahhh ... fuck-ing gahhhhd ..." I cried, not caring about how loud I shouted. "So ... fucking ... much ..."

I burst through a series of powerful spasms, hugging both dicks and shifting on Felix.

Henry came too, flooding me with semen.

Through my convulsions, it was only the constancy of the horizon that seemed to keep me sane, as a few layered, wispy clouds blurred with a range of hazy hills in the distance.

My body didn't feel like my own and I was shaking with bliss. Every nerve and every synapse overloaded with ecstasy. My vaginal and anal muscles had so much solid cock to grip each time they convulsed that the orgasm seemed to roll onwards, over and over, dragging me to the point of oblivion with each spasm.

"Jesus, that's … that's … incredible," Henry gasped.

I dug my nails into his shoulders, leaving my mark. He was mine. I was his. It was the way it was for us.

My pussy calmed though my ass remained tight as a noose around Felix's cock.

"You okay?" Henry asked, wiping at a bead of sweat on his brow.

"Yes."

The balloon suddenly tipped at our corner, not much, but enough to seat me even more fully onto Felix.

Felix groaned and tightened his grip on me. He hadn't come.

Henry pulled out and a gush of cum spilled out over his penis. Still, he didn't let me go, continuing to support my weight with Felix nestled in behind me.

"Felix," I gasped. "You didn't …"

"I'm so close," he said, giving my earlobe a little nip. "So damn close. Can you reach my balls … play with them. That'll finish me off in seconds … and fuck do I need to do that."

Sandwiched between them as I was, it seemed unlikely that I'd be able to oblige. But I reached down as best I could, trying to search out his heavy scrotum.

I couldn't reach, not at that angle.

But Felix groaned excitedly against my ear. "Yes … that's it … fuck. Yeah, like that, roll them like that. That's perfect."

I stared at Henry. I could feel his knuckles brushing

my thigh, my ass. *He* was fondling Felix.

Damn, and his face. He was looking straight at me. Delight and excitement searing through his eyes.

I'd just orgasmed, spectacularly, but seeing him, like that, fuck I could come all over again. It was one of the sexiest things I'd ever seen, Henry just giving into need, his need, Felix's need, my need and crossing the boundaries to deliver. I didn't think for a minute he was gay, but damn, if it felt good why the hell not?

Felix was still as a statue behind me. His ass-fucking was not the wild rut I'd expect from a man on the brink of orgasm. Rather, his calm and deliberate stokes, matched by his deep breathing told me he was taking in every sensation, taking in what I gave to him, taking what Henry gave him.

I clenched my ass around his penis and was rewarded with a guttural groan.

Henry kept fondling, leaned in and kissed me.

As our tongues tangled, Felix released his pent up fluid into the condom. Filling the skintight sheath, his shaft rippled in my rectum as he claimed his pleasure.

We all moaned and writhed, our sweat-sheened bodies forming a tangled mass against one another. Being sandwiched between two hot, filthy-minded, dirty-deed-doing, fantasy-fulfilling men was truly a dream come true.

"My god, that was amazing," Felix said from behind me, his voice still thick with lust. "I have to check our position."

"I think your position is pretty good," I said with a

giggle.

Henry slid his hands beneath my buttocks so that I was cradled in his arms. With one strong movement, he plucked me off of his friend and pulled me into his chest. Felix bucked and groaned as the tight ring of my ass squeezed over his softening, sensitive glans.

My ass and pussy felt empty but satisfied and they held a delicate warmth that intensified if I clamped. Henry set me down and I stood, nestled against his chest with my hands clasped beneath my chin, as he wrapped his arms around me.

Felix rushed, condom still in place, to the gas. He fired more heat into the balloon and then reached for the walkie-talkie.

"This is FF, Chase Crew FM please come in."

"The is Chase Crew FM, we can see you FF."

"They can see us?" I gasped and slapped my hands over my mouth.

Henry laughed. "Only from a long distance. Don't worry, we didn't give them a porno show."

"We'll start a descent in five," Felix said into the radio.

"Roger that, see you then."

"Over and out."

"We're going down?" I asked, moving to the side of the basket again. I was disappointed but at the same time, I was kind of looking forward to having Henry to myself again.

"What goes up must come down," Henry said, keeping me within his warm arms.

"I guess that's true," I said, wriggling against his cock and admiring a string of big houses, several of which had swimming pools. "Your cock goes up and down with amazing regularity."

"Only when I'm with you," he said. His voice quieted, became serious. "It's only you, Faye. You do understand that, don't you?"

I turned to face him.

His brow was creased and he was tugging on his bottom lip with his teeth.

"Yes," I said, "At least I hope that's how you feel."

He shook his head. "I think you've spoiled me for all others," he said. "I didn't think I was the settling down type, but these last six months ..."

"Go on?" My heart rate, which had indicated signs of steadying, was rapidly picking up pace again.

"These last six months, you've shown me that settling down, being with one person, well it's far from boring or monotonous. It's amazing, fascinating and exhilarating. Every emotion gets more intense, every sensation more wonderful as you get to know someone. Someone you're in perfect tune with."

He felt the same way I did. My heart soared. Had he been worrying that I was just enjoying a bit of fun with him? That I didn't feel anything for him beyond a fuck?

"Henry," I touched his face, moved another wayward

lock of hair. "Are you saying we've moved on from being fuck buddies to being in a relationship?"

"Yes, absolutely that's what I'm saying." He nodded vigorously. "If that's what you want of course."

I smiled and smoothed my palm down his jaw. "Yes, that's exactly what I want."

He let out a small sigh. "Thank heavens for that."

"Hey you two, you might want to don some clothes fairly soon," Felix said, ridding himself of the condom and reaching for his chinos.

"Yeah, yeah, in a minute," Henry cupped my face in his hands. "After I've kissed the girl I'm in love with."

HEAT

◇◇◇◇

STELLA HARRIS

H e a t

Zoe was at her wits end and things were only getting worse. She'd just taken the plunge and quit her job of five years, a job that made her miserable, only to find out that her husband was leaving her and she would be left with almost no income. If she stopped to think for more than a minute, she started to panic. It was only through sheer stubbornness that she didn't call up her old boss and ask for her job back, but she'd quit for a reason and was determined to stick with it.

Zoe was having what she called her early mid-life crisis. At only 29 years old she realized she didn't know what she wanted to be when she grew up. It was an unsettling feeling. Zoe had always prided herself on having a plan. Unfortunately that plan centered largely on financial stability; she'd neglected to consider happiness.

So here she was; eight months shy of her 30th birthday, jobless, and single.

Luckily Zoe had a network of supportive friends … the kind of friends that made enemies unnecessary. She knew they had her best interests in mind, but damn could they be pushy.

"Pass the wine, bitch." Daphne said, not waiting for Zoe to comply, but reaching across her in an awkward grab for the wine bottle.

"How many glasses is that for you now?" Zoe asked, wondering if she had clean bedding for the couch. It didn't look like Daphne would be in any shape to drive any time soon.

"I stopped counting at three, and that was a while ago."

Zoe sighed and rolled her eyes, but it was mostly for show. Daphne was one of her closest friends and Zoe would have been lost without her these last few weeks. Also, watching Daphne drink made Zoe feel better about her own wine consumption.

The project for tonight, at least according to Daphne, was to find a distraction for Zoe. Her suggestions had ranged from the horrible to the absurd, but apparently the wine was doing wonders, because her last few ideas weren't half bad.

"Something grassroots, small-scale, you know …" Okay, so maybe she wasn't at her most coherent, but Daphne had started making some good suggestions. Or maybe Zoe'd had enough to drink to *think* they were good suggestions.

"My facebook friend Gwen is always posting stuff about saving whales and seals and orphans, lets see what she's up to," Daphne said, executing another awkward grab, but this time for the laptop on the coffee table. A few clumsy keystrokes later Daphne started squealing, and Zoe was worried that her laptop was about to get doused with wine. "He's pretty, do this one," Daphne said, pointing at the screen with the hand just barely holding her wine glass.

Zoe used this excuse to take the laptop away from her and to see what had Daphne in such a tizzy. It seemed that her friend Gwen's latest cause was Haiti; there was a whole album of pictures of her work there. Zoe had sent money after the earthquake, but hadn't considered—even for a moment—actually going there. She didn't have any building or first aid skills, and she figured she'd just be in the way. Also, her idea of an adventure was something a little less dangerous. And a lot less hot and sticky. But Daphne was giving her that look that would not tolerate argument, so she kept looking at Gwen's page.

The picture that had gotten Daphne so riled up was of a whole volunteer group standing in front of a brightly colored building. Everyone was smiling. They also appeared sweaty and there were more than a few sun burns to be seen on the volunteers.

That said, the man that had Daphne so excited *was* pretty. So were most of the volunteers, actually. Who knew do-gooders were such an attractive bunch? But maybe that was the wine talking ...

Daphne started nudging into Zoe hard enough to threaten both of their wine glasses and Zoe knew she had to throw her a bone. "I'll look into it. Tomorrow. When I'm sober." Daphne squinted at her, as if trying to divine her sincerity, and eventually she grabbed for the tv remote and started trolling for a movie, so apparently Zoe had been convincing enough for now.

The next morning Zoe woke up cursing everything within sight, most especially the sun streaming through her curtains. Just as she was working up a murderous rage, Daphne came into the room with a steaming cup of coffee, and Zoe decided to postpone her murder spree until she'd had a sip or two. It was surprisingly good. She was feeling less stabby with each gulp.

"Why are you so perky?" Zoe was both suspicious and cranky that Daphne didn't seem to have a hangover.

"Practice, my dear. Years of practice. And also aspirin and water before bed," Daphne said with a wink. It was a good thing Zoe didn't want to spill her coffee or she might have given a second thought to that violent rampage.

"So, you going to sign up for that trip now?"

Zoe understood each of the words coming out of Daphne's mouth but had no idea what she was saying. Her look must have conveyed as much.

"The volunteer trip to Haiti?" Daphne nudged. "The registration deadline is tomorrow, no time to waste!" Daphne added in a sing-song voice as she left the room. "Get dressed, we've got to go shopping. You're going to need a whole new wardrobe for this." Daphne's voice carried incredibly well and Zoe's head throbbed with it. It almost seemed worth agreeing if it meant Daphne would let her go back to sleep.

Zoe supposed taking a trip wasn't so outlandish after all. She could use the change of scenery—it would probably help clear her mind. Everything around the house reminded her of her old job or her ex-husband. Things she was working on forgetting—or at least forgetting for a few minutes at a time.

She had enough savings to coast for a little while, and as selfish as it sounded, maybe helping other people with their problems would help her stop thinking about her own. More importantly, a trip like that would help her gain some much needed perspective.

Zoe managed to ward off most of Daphne's shopping suggestions, but she had caved and bought a new bathing suit. Short of that, she couldn't justify a new wardrobe to do volunteer work. She wasn't going on this trip for a photo op, she was going to do some real good. And if going on a trip did her some good too, all the better.

The house seemed unnaturally quiet now that Daphne had gone home. A week of having her come and go from the house had distracted Zoe and she'd almost forgotten that she lived alone now. Evenings were the hardest; the time between having dinner and going to bed. When all of her tasks for the day were done and she finally started slowing down she had time to think. Zoe still wasn't ready to spend much time thinking.

In the aftermath of Daphne's visit there were wine bottles scattered around the house, with a few unfinished bottles in the fridge. Zoe decided to take advantage of not wanting to waste any wine to bypass her rule against drinking alone.

With a glass of freshly poured wine in hand, Zoe grabbed her laptop from where it had been abandoned on the coffee table. When she opened it, she saw the picture they'd looked at the night before. Even sober, the people in the picture were especially pretty. Her eyes fell once more on the man Daphne had been so excited about. He wasn't really Zoe's type, but it was probably time she developed a new type. There was no guarantee he'd be on the trip she took, but for one night at least it didn't hurt to dream.

Zoe took her glass of wine into her bedroom to get ready for bed. She undressed, leaving her clothes on the dresser while eyeing her shopping bag from that day. The bathing suit she'd gotten was fairly conservative by western standards but it looked good on her. The simple black suit made the most of Zoe's pale skin and the cut of the waist gave her more of an hourglass than she usually had.

Zoe imagined herself stepping out of a pool, dripping wet, with the man from the picture watching her. Would his eyes fall to the way the suit accentuated the curve of her breast, or would he be more of a legs and ass man? Zoe's nipples hardened under the imagined scrutiny. She could almost feel the chill from the pool water evaporating from her skin, before the sun could dry and warm her. Zoe's body felt alive in a way it hadn't for months, just the thought of breaking out of her routine was enough to make her feel exhilarated.

As she finished undressing, Zoe pulled a satin nightshirt over her head. The feel of the soft fabric against her already hard nipples gave her a shudder and she sighed. Even sliding under the covers made her nerves light up with sensation.

Zoe grabbed her wine glass from the nightstand and took another sip. She let the wine sit in her mouth a moment before swallowing, savoring the taste. When she set the wine back down she eyed the drawer in her nightstand. She hadn't opened that drawer for a while …

Zoe emptied the rest of the wine into her mouth and opened the drawer. In it sat her favorite purple vibrator; the only toy she liked enough to give bedside status. Others were relegated to a box at the bottom of her closet.

With the vibrator clutched tightly, Zoe slid her hand under the covers and between her legs. She turned the vibrator to its lowest setting and closed her eyes, letting the sensation wash over her. She let her mind drift back to her fantasy of the handsome man by the pool. Maybe he'd be waiting for her with a towel, maybe he'd hand her a drink, or maybe he'd wait for her to lie down and he'd rub her shoulders.

Zoe bet he'd have strong hands—he must if he did construction work. She wondered if they'd be rough and callused, making her shiver when they brushed against her skin, or if he managed to keep his hands smooth and soft. She wasn't sure which idea she liked better so she just focused on the thought of his hands exploring her body, working her sore muscles until they began to release the tension she'd been carrying around for months.

Zoe could feel her shoulders relaxing and she let her legs fall open. She turned the vibrator up and arched her hips against it rhythmically. In her mind the handsome man continued his exploration of her body, and suddenly they were in a hotel room rather than by the pool. Fantasies were convenient that way.

He slid the straps of the bathing suit off her shoulders and pulled the suit completely off Zoe's body. Her damp skin broke out in goosebumps when exposed to the air and his touch gave them reason to stay. When the palms of his hands brushed against her nipples Zoe came so hard she actually cried out—that rarely happened when she was alone. Zoe surprised herself, she didn't usually come so quickly. She hadn't even gotten to the good part of the fantasy.

Oh, well. There would be plenty of time for that on the trip. At least that's what she told herself while drifting off to sleep.

The next few days passed in a whirlwind of packing and planning to go away. Daphne, of course, volunteered to water her plants and feed her fish. As Zoe went through her checklist of preparations, she couldn't help thinking that Daphne was a little surprised that she was actually going through with the trip. Hopefully this wouldn't encourage Daph to be any more pushy. She was already threatening to set Zoe up with a dating site profile.

When Zoe found the right gate at the airport, she must have looked wide-eyed and lost, because one of the group leaders came right up to her. She could tell he was a group leader because he wore a bright yellow t-shirt emblazoned with the words, "GROUP LEADER."

"Hi, I'm Scott, are you with the Haitian Sun group?" It wasn't until she heard his voice that Zoe managed to look away from his blinding attire to find herself looking right at the handsome man from Gwen's pictures. Zoe was at a loss for words. All the dirty thoughts she'd had about this man began to flash through her mind and she was sure she was bushing. She opened her mouth to introduce herself and closed it again, not sure she could speak without her voice cracking. This was not the first impression she'd hoped to make.

When his expression shifted from welcome to concern, she snapped out of her reverie. "Yes, that's right. I'm Zoe," she said, offering a hand. He ignored the hand and hugged her. This left one of her arms awkwardly between them for the hug. Yup, things were off to a great start.

"Our group is sitting over here," Scott said, gesturing to a group of people sitting in chairs and on the floor. Zoe thought a couple other faces looked familiar from the pictures but she couldn't be sure. No one else was wearing a neon shirt.

A few people were re-packing their luggage,

consolidating donations and making sure everything vital fit in their carry-on bags. This was enough to rekindle Zoe's packing anxiety, but she shoved those concerns down as best as she could. She loved visiting new places, but the transportation in between she could do without. Zoe was the type of person who stressed about details. Daphne would say she stressed about everything. Zoe preferred to think of herself as detail oriented.

This attention to detail made flying especially stressful for her. Not to mention her actual fear of flying. At least the worry of forgetting something meant that she didn't start worrying about the plane falling out of the sky until she was sitting on it. By then it was too late.

But no one else in the group looked the least bit concerned and Zoe was here for a new experience and a new perspective. What better way to start than to let their calm demeanor wash over her?

Zoe's commitment to calm lasted about ten minutes into the flight. She passed the relatively short trip white knuckled and in the company of religious missionaries. Zoe tried to explain that the volunteer trip she was on wasn't church related, but was met with only confusion on the part of her seat-mate. Still, the stilted conversation provided some distraction from the constant turbulence, and Zoe was grateful for any distraction she could get.

When they landed in Port au Prince she was tempted to thank any gods listening, but her flying companions had spoiled that impulse for her. Instead she focused on grabbing her bag from the overhead bin and not utterly losing her group. Luckily Scott was tall, so she just kept an eye out for his head bouncing above the crowd—and for flashes of bright yellow.

The second Zoe stepped off of the plane she was hit by a wall of humidity and heat. That's exactly what it felt like—a wall. She had to brace herself and consciously step forward. Like walking into a sauna but without the promise of a cold dunking pool just steps away when she'd had too much.

The room they were herded into was unlike any airport Zoe had seen before. She found herself in a big open space with several baggage carousels, a few customs booths, and hundreds of people; many of them shouting in Creole. There were also guards and airport staff in uniform walking around and one was collecting passports from everyone in Zoe's group.

Everything took her a few extra moments to process. The air felt too thick to breathe. Zoe's hair stuck to her forehead and she could feel drops of sweat collecting between her breasts.

Zoe's previous travels had taught her never to part with her passport, but everyone in her group was handing theirs over and she could see Scott smiling so she went with the flow. There was too much to take in, she couldn't process it all. She saw the missionaries from her flight along with other organized groups and many people she assumed were

Haitian, returning from their travels.

The next hour was a haze of jostling bodies; lining up in one place and then lining up in another. She just followed the crowd and focused on breathing. Zoe portioned out sips from the flimsy plastic water bottle she'd been handed and tried to ignore the faint chemical taste.

Zoe was perhaps the last to realize what awaited them next. She was so relieved to have her bags with her again and to exit the airport that she hadn't paused to consider that they weren't staying in Port au Prince, but rather in a small coastal town. Why hadn't she wondered about the last leg of the trip before?

When Zoe stood beside the tiny plane that would take them to their final destination she cursed Daphne for talking her into this trip along with anyone else she could think of whose fault it was she was here; her ex-husband and her ex-boss made the list several times.

It took all the willpower in Zoe's body to get onto the plane—and really, 'plane' was a generous description. The outside of the questionable aircraft was painted in bright yellow letters and a dotted line that read, "cut here to break in." This gave her no confidence whatsoever.

It was only Scott's smiling face and offered hand that made her walk up the wobbly stairs. She took the seat next to him and was determined to put on a brave act. Oh, the things she put up with for a pretty face.

When they landed for the second time that day they

were herded into vans and driven to the hotel. If it weren't for the horror of the flight she'd just endured, she would have been scared silly by the conditions on the road, but for now she was just grateful to be so close to solid ground.

When they disembarked at the hotel, Zoe was stunned. It was absolutely breathtaking. Nothing she'd seen so far had prepared her for something so lovely. She hadn't really considered where she'd be staying, but a tropical paradise certainly hadn't crossed her mind.

The building was a soft peach color with open, sloped entryways. The floors were intricate tile work and flowered vines draped over every surface. Stepping into the lobby she saw that the beauty continued. Every point in the hotel had an ocean view that would have been at home on any postcard.

As much as Zoe wanted to take everything in, she was also exhausted. She could see that the other members of the group looked tired too. She hoped they didn't have anything planned for that evening.

"Is this your first time?" Zoe turned around to see a small blonde woman looking at her.

"Excuse me?" were the first words that came to her mouth. At least Zoe was consistent, if nothing else. She wouldn't want to ruin her perfect record of bad first impressions.

"Your first time in Haiti I mean. I'm Megan, by the way." Megan said, offering her hand and a bright smile. Zoe couldn't remember if Megan had been one of the people in the picture but she shook her hand and smiled in return.

"Yes, it's my first time," Zoe said, looking around as she answered. There was a lot to take in.

"Not what you were expecting?"

"I don't know what I was expecting, to be honest. I didn't put a lot of thought into it. I just wanted to do something completely different," Zoe said, leaving the wine, the pushy friend, and the lustful thoughts out of her answer.

Zoe was saved from answering any follow-up questions by Scott handing over a room key. "Zoe, Megan, are you two okay rooming together?" Scott asked. Among the many things Zoe hadn't considered was sharing a room, but she supposed Megan was as good as anyone. Well, anyone but Scott. But she was hardly going to suggest that.

"Absolutely!" Megan answered, with alarming enthusiasm. She grabbed her key and her bags and rushed off in the direction of the room. Zoe looked at Scott with wide eyes. She wasn't sure she could handle that kind of exuberance for a whole week. Megan was probably a morning person, too.

"I thought it would be good for you to room with a seasoned volunteer," Scott explained, seeing Zoe's worried look. It was a perfect opening to suggest she room with him but even her travel-addled mind had enough sense to keep quiet.

"Great, thanks," she said instead and, with a weak smile, followed her cheerleader of a roommate towards what would be home for the next few days.

Once Zoe saw the size of the bed that would be hers, all was forgiven. All she wanted at that moment was to curl up and sleep for about twelve hours. Hopefully Megan could take her enthusiasm elsewhere.

Zoe must have gotten her wish because the next thing she knew she was opening her eyes to a new day. Sure, it was earlier than she would have liked but at least she'd gone to bed early. Of course, Zoe would have preferred a wake-up that didn't involve Megan singing and dancing around the room, but her good mood was contagious and Zoe was eager to see what the day held.

When it came time to divide tasks, Zoe volunteered for the group Scott was leading without hearing what project they'd be working on. She did, however, notice that Megan had chosen a different group. In fact, most of the volunteers chose different groups. Zoe might have worried if she wasn't too preoccupied by the thought of spending the day with Scott. She didn't have a crush, she told herself. She didn't know him well enough for that. But he was beautiful eye-candy and that was just what Zoe needed.

A few hours later it was official. Zoe had a crush.

It would have been easy to dismiss her lust if Scott had just been a pretty face, but after spending the morning together hauling rocks, it turned out he was a wonderful person too.

Thanks to the rest of the group being more alert in the morning than Zoe, most people chose tasks like painting, cleaning, or working with children. Zoe had volunteered to move rocks. In the sun. In one-hundred degree weather. At least it was good exercise.

This also meant she finally had time to talk to Scott and learn more about him and what he was doing here.

"I came down here for the first time right after the earthquake. My company sent me as part of a PR campaign. They were donating staff time but no money. So I was stuck here making recommendations to people who couldn't afford to implement them. What good is it to tell people how to build a safer school without any money or materials? When I got home from the trip I knew I had to do something. So after a few phone calls I quit my job and started Haitian Sun." Scott had been talking for a long time and Zoe was happy to just listen. She asked a few questions here and there so he'd know she was paying attention, but mostly she just wanted to listen to him talk.

Not only was he beautiful, he was a decent human being. Fed up with his corporate job (much like she had been) he stepped up to make a difference. Zoe wanted to find parallels between them but there was a big difference between starting a non-profit and just attending a volunteer trip.

"This is my tenth trip and the progress amazes me every time," Scott finished. Okay, so maybe Zoe had stopped paying attention. In her defense, Scott was very distracting. She couldn't stop looking at the way the muscles moved under the skin of his arms as he lifted the heaviest rocks—

saving the smaller ones for her—or the way his eyes twinkled in the bright sun.

Zoe hadn't failed to notice that most of the volunteers on the trip were women and she was beginning to wonder how much Scott's special brand of charm had to do with that.

"I think it's time for lunch," Scott said. Zoe realized she was hungry as soon as he spoke. Heavy lifting was a great way to work up an appetite, even if she wasn't doing the worst of it.

The rest of the group was back at the hotel already when Zoe and Scott arrived. The van had come back for them last and when Zoe finally sat down to eat she was starving. Although the meals they were served were different from what she'd make herself at home, she was fast warming to the local cuisine. Beans and rice were served at every meal and there was usually fresh fish and fruit, too. There were benefits to being on a tropical island. The fruit juices alone were worth the trip.

After lunch several people planned to go swimming; and after her dirty, sweaty morning that sounded like a great plan. Zoe went back to her room to change into her new bathing suit and couldn't help but wonder if Scott would be down there. The similarities to her fantasies also made her feel a little dirty, but that couldn't be helped.

When she'd changed and grabbed a towel, Zoe went down to the pool and saw Megan sitting with her feet dangling in the water. Megan gave her a big smile and a wave as Zoe walked over to the pool and stepped in. The water felt amazing. It wasn't exactly cool, but by comparison to the air it was incredibly refreshing. She'd hardly realized how baked she'd gotten under the sun until she felt the pool envelop her. Between the food, the view, and now the pool, this was starting to feel more like a vacation than volunteer work.

The next morning, Zoe paid more attention when tasks were being allocated. As much as she'd enjoyed her alone time with Scott, she hadn't enjoyed it enough to move rocks two days in a row. Instead she chose working on art projects at a school—that seemed like the most relaxing option offered that day. She didn't have much artistic talent, but she wasn't going to let that stop her.

When they walked into the school Zoe thought maybe she should reconsider. From the art on the walls she could see these kids had real talent and she had no idea what she could offer them. However Scott and the other volunteers were already heading out to their own assignments and Zoe couldn't back out now.

"Meet us back at the hotel later?" Scott asked, and flashed his charming smile.

Zoe was so determined to look like she had her act together she answered, "Sure," before having any idea how she'd actually do that.

"Great, see you at dinner!" Scott said before hopping

back into the van and driving away. Zoe considered her surroundings forlornly before being distracted by a child tugging on her arm. She looked down to see an adorable little girl who stood about as tall as Zoe's waist impatiently trying to get her attention.

"Kisa?" Zoe said, glad for the time she'd spent practicing with the Haitian Creole app on her phone. The girl answered in long sentences Zoe had no hope of understanding, but the message was clear; the girl was trying to get Zoe to follow her. Having no idea what else to do, she complied.

Deploying another phrase from her app, Zoe asked, "Kouman ou rélé?" figuring if they were going to spend time together, she should call the girl by her name.

"Melyssa," the girl answered with a smile, seemingly happy to communicate.

"Mwen rélé Zoe," Zoe said, becoming concerned that she was close to the limits of her Creole.

It took Melyssa a couple of tries to pronounce 'Zoe' correctly, but when she did the smile Zoe received for complementing her was well worth it.

Having reached their destination, Zoe saw she'd been led to a craft table. Apparently her new friend would have multiple reasons to be disappointed. She'd seen the art these kids created and there was no way her own talents were up to par. Melyssa waived away Zoe's protestations, although she couldn't have understood exactly what Zoe was saying.

Before Zoe knew it she was up to her elbows in

paper maché and having the time of her life. Although her creatures weren't coming out as nicely as Melyssa's, they were both having fun and nothing else seemed to matter. Their communication barriers were long forgotten as instructions, advice and questions were all conveyed with gestures and hands. If it hadn't been for the children getting called in for dinner, Zoe wouldn't even have thought to check the time.

When she saw it was nearly six, she knew she'd better return to the problem of how she was going to get back to the hotel. She said farewell to her crafting companion and exited the school compound. Once on the street, the reality of her situation began to sink back in. She'd seen people flag down motorcycles and hop on the back; it seemed to be the local version of a taxi. But in flip-flops and a skirt, she was hardly dressed for that mode of transportation.

Still, Zoe's decision was made for her when a man pulled up in front of her on his motorbike. He asked her something she couldn't understand and she hoped he was asking where she wanted to go—because that's the answer she gave. She had to say the name of the hotel three times before being understood. With that, she climbed awkwardly onto the back of the bike, tried to tuck her legs up out of the way, and hung on for dear life.

If possible, this was even more terrifying than the small plane ride had been. The motorcycle kept swerving around traffic and the unpaved road made for a bumpy ride. Zoe's skirt and flip-flops were certainly not the best attire for this mode of transportation and if she didn't pull a muscle hanging on she'd count herself lucky.

Zoe's heart was racing and if it hadn't been for several firm bites to her bottom lip she probably would have screamed or at least let fly a few choice curse words. She thought of every movie that made fun of traffic in New York or Los Angeles and wanted to tell them they didn't know what they were talking about. You haven't seen traffic until you've seen someone riding a motorbike with a rooster under one arm and a pig beneath the other.

The bike took an especially sharp turn and Zoe thought for sure they would tip over. The driver steadied the bike by reaching out and holding them up with his hand on the truck next to them—a technique that would have panicked Zoe further if she hadn't just found a fantastic distraction.

As the bike had tipped, she'd lost her balance and her foot had left the bike to catch her fall by stepping onto the ground. Unfortunately, this meant she'd rested her ankle squarely on the bike's tailpipe, and it took a moment for the signals reaching her brain to tell her she was getting burned. Zoe pulled her foot out of the way as quickly as she could but the damage was already done. The bike had started moving again and she couldn't get a good look, but from her vantage point she was pretty sure a nasty blister was already forming.

When they reached the hotel she stepped off the bike unsteadily and paid the driver. That near death experience only cost her a dollar—a bargain by any estimation. Zoe squatted to get a better look at her ankle and it wasn't good.

She had a blister at least three inches across forming on the inside of her ankle and it was already filling with fluid. She'd brought bandages with her, but nothing appropriate for treating a burn. So much for looking like she had her act together.

Accepting an additional injury, this time to her pride, Zoe limped over to Scott's room. He seemed like the kind of guy who would be prepared for emergencies. Apparently he was also the kind of guy who would open his hotel room door without putting on a shirt. Zoe decided to blame her latest loss of words on the pain she was in, rather than the sight of Scott's bare chest.

"I had an accident," Zoe eventually managed to say, pointing lamely towards her ankle. Scott looked confused for only a moment before squatting down at her feet for a closer look.

"That's a pretty nasty burn. Come in," he said, already moving backwards into his room.

Scott disappeared into the bathroom and Zoe took a moment to look around her. Like every other room she'd seen the view was amazing. There wasn't a single cloud in the sky, just blue as far as the eye could see.

Scott came back into the room a moment later with his arms full of first aid supplies. "Sit," he told her, and she did. He began work immediately, taking her foot into his lap. His hands were soothing against her calf. His skin somehow felt cool even though the air was still at least 95 degrees. It felt like each of his touches lingered for longer than necessary, but perhaps her injury had made her over-sensitive.

"How does that feel," he asked, and it took Zoe's mind a moment to catch up and realize he meant the bandage, not his hand on her leg.

"Good. Better. Much better," she stammered, trying to catch herself before giving too much away. Considering the glint in his eye, she had probably failed.

"You're cute when you're nervous," Scott said, and Zoe was pretty sure she blushed. Although already flushed from the heat, it was hard to tell.

"So, that would be all the time then?" At least she had snark to fall back on, and as he laughed she felt the tension break.

"Yeah, pretty much," he said, and brushed a strand of sweat-damp hair behind her ear. Being sweaty normally made her feel gross, but in this instance the word 'sultry' came to mind. Between the flush, the sweat, and the mussed hair, she was walking around looking freshly-fucked most of the time. Apparently the look was working for her.

His face was next to hers, nuzzling her ear, before she'd realized he'd moved. It had been a while since she'd been close to someone and it felt good. She let herself lean against him and when his tongue snaked out to tickle her ear, she placed a hand on his shoulder and squeezed.

Zoe turned her face until her lips could find Scott's and she kissed him deeply. She longed to reach out and touch his body but wasn't sure how far to take this. She hadn't exactly planned for this to happen—she hadn't even packed condoms.

"Won't we be late for dinner?" Once again, Zoe spoke without thinking. She wanted to kick herself as soon as the words were out of her mouth, but Scott's amused look made her feel better.

"You're right, the rest of the group is probably missing us."

To Zoe's dismay she didn't get another chance to be alone with Scott that night. She noticed him looking at her a couple times during dinner and she got such a thrill out of it she felt like a schoolgirl. She'd forgotten how much she enjoyed flirting.

The next day was just as hectic and Zoe wondered if she'd ever get Scott alone again. As lunch was breaking up Zoe decided to follow Scott for the afternoon no matter what he was working on. She was willing to do whatever it took to get another kiss, even if that meant moving more rocks.

As they headed towards the parking lot, a beautiful woman walked up to the group. She had long red hair, a freckled face, and looked perfectly at ease in the blazing sun. Scott greeted her with a hug and a kiss on the cheek. Zoe hadn't decided if she should be jealous yet when Scott turned back to the group to introduce the newcomer.

"Everyone, I want you to meet my wife, Grace." Scott's words were met with a rumble of greetings from the volunteers who still stood with them but Zoe was left hoping she'd heard wrong.

"Your wife?" Zoe thought that she'd thought it, but it turned out she'd spoken aloud. And now she wasn't sure what to be more indignant about. The fact that Scott had used her to cheat, or the fact that he seemed so casual about it. Everyone in the group turned to look at Zoe and that shut her up fast. Scott looked more amused than alarmed and that just pissed her off even more.

"Yes, that's right. Grace runs the Haitian Sun program with me but doesn't attend all of the trips," Scott explained, but Zoe wasn't paying close attention.

"What he's not saying is that I usually stay home and do the paperwork," Grace said, flashing a smile. She seemed utterly charming but Zoe didn't want to be charmed, she wanted to be mad.

Sadly, that was going to have to wait. Everyone was piling into vans for the day's projects and Zoe had made a big enough scene already. She stewed in her thoughts during the ride and thus found herself at the last stop with Scott and Grace. She should have gotten off somewhere else—now she'd be stuck with them for hours.

The project that morning was building houses. Simple, one room houses, but houses nonetheless. They were a big step up from the tents people were living in and Zoe managed to lose herself to the work. Although she still didn't have any construction skills to speak of, she could follow directions, move pieces of wood, and hold them where she was told.

She'd worked up a good sweat almost immediately

and after less than an hour she could feel the burn in her arms. Physical exertion was a great way to clear the mind and by the time she had a chance to focus on Scott and Grace again she wasn't mad anymore.

When the wall she'd been working on was done Zoe walked to the other side of the building to see if anyone else needed help. It was a good thing she'd gotten over her anger because Scott and Grace were working together on the other wall. Zoe watched as Grace and Scott worked side by side. They hardly needed to speak, one handing the other a tool without needing to be asked. It was remarkable.

Zoe could see why they were a couple. Grace and Scott seemed well matched on a number of levels. Aside from both being magazine beautiful, Grace was clearly as philanthropic as Scott was. Zoe wondered what job Grace had left to do this work.

Zoe also had to admire Grace's carpentry skills. She actually seemed to know what she was doing and she looked happy doing it.

That wasn't all Zoe was admiring. Zoe's eyes traced the way Grace's t-shirt clung to her body, hugging each and every one of Grace's curves. Zoe took no small satisfaction from seeing Grace break a sweat—even if she did manage to make it look elegant. At 107 degrees Zoe was dripping wet, and there was nothing elegant about it. Grace simply glistened. Zoe watched as a drop of sweat left Grace's hairline and trickled down the back of her neck. Zoe licked her lips as she imagined tasting that drop, imagined kissing it off Grace's skin.

Wait. What? Getting over being mad was one thing but now she was lusting over both of them? The heat must have been doing a number on her libido.

Still, if Grace and Scott were as coordinated during other tasks as they were doing construction ...

"What?" Zoe asked, realizing she'd missed something. Scott was looking at her with that infuriating amused grin and, although Grace wasn't looking, she was smiling. Zoe wondered how long he'd been trying to get her attention.

"Could you pass me the hammer?" Scott said, and Zoe hoped it was only for the second time.

Scott looked good in the sun, too. In this light Zoe saw that Grace wasn't the only one with freckles, although Scott's tan hid them well. The way his shirt pulled across his chest he looked like something out of an underwear advertisement. Solidifying the effect, Scott pulled up his shirt to wipe his face, displaying his firm stomach. Zoe's mouth went dry, but maybe that was just the heat. She grabbed her water and took a long sip, almost choking on it, to the continued amusement of both Scott and Grace.

This was ridiculous. "I'm going to go do something ... over there," Zoe said, floundering and pointing in the general direction of another project.

"Okay, but can I have the hammer first?" Scott asked, and now Zoe could see Grace's shoulders shaking. She was being laughed at, but she deserved it. You'd think she was a teenager again for how twitterpated these two had gotten her.

Zoe did a fantastic job of keeping busy for the rest of the day with her back to Scott and Grace. She wasn't mad any more—far from it—but she didn't trust herself holding tools with those two distracting her. She'd already had one injury on this trip, she didn't need another one.

When it was time to break for the day Zoe had managed to put together a bed frame all by herself and it didn't look half bad. More importantly, it was sturdy. It may have taken her twice as long as it would have taken someone else, but she wasn't going to let that diminish her pride.

"Good job," Scott said, patting her on the shoulder and he walked past her towards the van that had come to pick them up. Grace followed after him giving Zoe a smile as she went. Zoe glowed under their praise and attention and had to remind herself to move her feet and follow them to the van.

Separated by several other volunteers, Zoe didn't get a chance to talk to Scott and Grace at dinner; and afterward a local band came to play at the hotel. Perhaps it was just as well—some things should stay fantasies.

Zoe didn't usually dance but the band was getting to her. Or maybe it was the rum. The hotel made a damn good rum punch. It was a little different every time she ordered one, but the common element was that each cocktail was delicious.

By her third cocktail Zoe was really dancing, moving

her feet and everything. As she moved to the music she watched Scott and Grace dancing together and focused on how well they moved. As with everything else they did, they seemed perfectly in tune with each other. They moved so smoothly that Zoe didn't initially notice that they'd come to flank her, each dancing on either side of her body. She should have been embarrassed but the music, the booze, and the warm night air had put Zoe in a rare mood. She just kept dancing and let herself believe she was as graceful as them.

When Grace took her by the hand and began to lead her away, it seemed like a natural part of the dance and Zoe followed without a second thought. Before she knew it they'd arrived at Scott's room—which was now Scott and Grace's room—and she was being led inside. Zoe sat on the bed and Grace and Scott continued to flank her, one sitting on either side.

"Scott told me about the other night," Grace said, and Zoe's good mood began to falter.

"I should have told you I was married first," Scott added. "But I hadn't planned on kissing you, it just happened."

"I'm usually the communicator. Scott is more about action," Grace said, nudging Scott as she spoke. They were so adorable together it was hard to be uncomfortable.

That, and Zoe kept getting distracted as she looked at Grace. Her wavy red hair should have been a frazzled mess in this humidity and yet it fell perfectly around her face and down her shoulders. Speaking of her face, Grace wasn't sweating or flushed. Grace and Scott looked like they belonged on a soap opera, not in the middle of the poorest country in the western hemisphere.

Zoe was pulled back into the moment by Grace's hand on her knee. She looked down at the well manicured hand first, and then at Grace's face. The expression she found there was impassive—Zoe felt like Grace was trying to get a read on her.

"Speaking of action, it's only fair that I get even," Grace said. Zoe was starting to realize that Grace's poker face held a bit of mischief. It was hard to tell if Grace was serious or not—until their lips met.

Apparently Grace was serious.

Grace's lips, like the rest of her, were perfect. Smooth and soft, they pressed against Zoe's chapped lips and Zoe kissed back. When Grace's tongue nudged against her mouth Zoe immediately parted her lips to allow Grace entry.

Zoe could have happily kissed Grace all night, but Grace seemed to have other ideas. She moved to Zoe's neck and started kissing and biting. Zoe nuzzled into the curls behind Grace's ear and felt perfectly content.

Through heavy eyes, Zoe saw that Scott was watching them with an affectionate smile. Zoe's eyes closed and she felt his hands on her body, gliding over her shoulders and down her sides. If she'd been any less relaxed his touch would have tickled, but now it just melted her even further into a happy puddle.

Zoe hadn't overestimated Scott and Grace's ability to

work well together. While their mouths distracted her, their hands undressed her and she was naked between them in no time. As much as she loved being the center of attention, she wasn't going to let this night pass without getting a chance to enjoy their bodies too.

"Off," Zoe said, tugging at Grace's shirt. She didn't even try to be smooth about it. Grace chuckled and complied, and in a moment she was topless. She hadn't been wearing a bra—that explained why her breasts had been so mesmerizing when she danced. Grace's breasts were larger than Zoe's, full and perky with dark nipples already hard and wrinkled.

Deciding she'd been passive for long enough, Zoe pushed Grace back onto the bed and took one prominent nipple into her mouth. There was the faintest taste of salt from the sheen that lightly coated Grace's whole body, and Zoe sucked the flavor off of her. Grace writhed beneath her and Zoe held her wrists down to keep her still. She'd been looking at this body all day and she wasn't going to miss her chance to explore it. Grace started making the most delicious sounds and Zoe sucked harder. She was glad Grace's nipples were so sensitive, she was going to have a lot of fun with this.

The act of kneeling over Grace had pushed Zoe's own ass, proud and exposed, up into the air. Scott accepted her tacit invitation and began exploring her ass and her hips with his hands. His touch was joyfully distracting, and she waggled her butt at him to let him know. She heard his low chuckle a second before his fingers parted her ass cheeks and his tongue followed.

Zoe gasped and flinched, no one had ever done this to her before. Any words of protest she might have managed were silenced as Scott's fingers slid into her happy pussy. It was only Grace's insistent wiggle that reminded Zoe she was supposed to be focusing on something else right now.

As an apology for her distraction, Zoe moved lower on Grace's body and pulled her skirt up and out of the way. A bra wasn't the only undergarment she'd skipped; all the better for what Zoe had in mind. Zoe took a moment to admire how neatly trimmed and shaved Grace was, sparing a thought for all the things said about redheads, before leaning forward and licking a long line up Grace's pretty slit.

Grace gasped and pressed her hips forward, burying Zoe's face even deeper, and Zoe didn't mind one bit. As she licked at Grace, Scott's fingers and tongue worked at her, and she lost herself to the feedback loop of pleasure.

Grace tasted delicious, and the longer Zoe worked on her the more completely Grace's tastes and smells overcame the lingering haze of rum cocktails. This was an intoxication of another kind.

Zoe's circuits were ready to overload. Every time Scott did something that felt especially good she'd get lost in the feeling only to be brought back on task by Grace's bucking hips or grasping hands. Zoe knew Grace was close when she got an even tighter grip on her hair and refused to let go. Grace wasn't going to let Zoe get distracted again.

Zoe fought against the pleasure she was experiencing

to focus on Grace. Once she'd given Grace what she needed, Zoe could focus on her own pleasure.

Grace was easy to read. Her moans, gasps, and encouraging 'yesses' led Zoe to all the things Grace liked best. When Zoe found a rhythm and pressure that was working, Grace pulled so hard on her hair that it hurt, but Zoe wasn't going to stop. The pain heightened her focus, and her own pleasure, and she worked diligently with her tongue, eager to coax an orgasm out of Grace.

She didn't have to wait long. With one more tug on her hair, Grace pulled Zoe face-first into her cunt. Grace bucked and seized and shuddered on the bed as a flood of moisture hit Zoe's face. There was so much wetness that Zoe might have laughed if she wasn't worried about the very real possibility of drowning.

When Grace let go of her hair Zoe came up for air with a few desperate gasps. She could think of worse ways to die, but she certainly wanted her own orgasm first. She grabbed her discarded shirt to wipe her face and then rested her head in Grace's lap to relax and focus on the things Scott was doing to her.

His tongue had penetrated her ass and she couldn't keep her hips still. She was bucking forward and back which drove his fingers in and out of her even faster. Zoe could have climbed out of her skin for want of an orgasm, but Grace's arms enveloped her shoulders and held her tight; grounding her in her own body.

Suddenly, Scott's thumb flicked across Zoe's clit and

that was all it took, she convulsed and her cunt grabbed at Scott's fingers as his tongue gave a last wiggle and pulled out. Zoe was still twitching as she collapsed on the bed.

Scott stood, took a long drink from a bottle of water, and then lay back on the bed. His cock stood straight up and Zoe's pulse raced with the overwhelming urge to ride him. A quick glance at Grace was met with a nod of approval as Grace produced a condom and handed it to Scott.

Although she'd been quite ready to die happily a moment before, Scott's naked and erect form was enough to give anyone a second wind. Zoe eagerly propped herself up on her still shaking legs and straddled Scott. She was still so wet that he slid right into her, despite his intimidating size.

Zoe leaned back and rested her hands on Scott's thighs behind her. She arched her back and savored the feeling of Scott thrusting up into her. She felt the bed dip, and Zoe opened her eyes to see Grace rise up and straddle Scott's face.

Face to face now with Zoe, Grace seemed intent on taking full advantage of the position. She leaned forward and captured Zoe's mouth in a kiss while her hands roamed over Zoe's body.

If his moans were any indication, Scott didn't mind being pinned beneath two women. His hips continued to thrust against Zoe and his hands came to rest on Grace's hips, holding her close to his face. This left Grace and Zoe with their hands free to touch, tease, and explore, as Scott reciprocated their pleasure below.

Grace pinched at Zoe's nipples with one hand while the other found its way back into Zoe's hair. Grabbing a fistful of tresses, Grace held Zoe in place for a deep kiss that felt like it lasted forever. They might never have stopped kissing if it hadn't been for Scott, whose urgent convulsions reclaimed their attention. With a final thrust and a loud cry he was spent, and Zoe and Grace reluctantly climbed off of his slackening, perspiring body.

Zoe found herself in the middle of a happy snuggle pile, with more hands touching her body than she could focus on at once. With so many combinations and positions to try, they would be at this for a while.

The next morning at breakfast Zoe received a raised-eyebrow greeting from Megan. Her absence from their room the night before had been noted, but the raised eyebrow was the extent of it. No comments were made, no questions asked.

They'd managed to get a couple hours sleep, but Zoe knew she'd be dragging that day. They still had a couple days of work left and she wanted to make sure that her nighttime activities didn't render her useless during the days.

Zoe counted down the remainder of the trip hour by hour. She'd gotten used to the schedule, the work, and even the heat, and she wasn't looking forward to returning to real life. She thought of the empty house that waited for her, with only a fish for company. She thought of the dozens of emails she'd likely have from well-meaning friends, forwarding her listings of jobs that she didn't want to do.

Most of all she thought about Scott and Grace and how at ease she felt with them, and how good it felt for her time and effort to be making a real difference.

On the last morning, as everyone was dragging their luggage into the lobby, Scott and Grace approached Zoe. "What's your plan when you get home?" Grace asked. Between bouts of aerobic sex Zoe had managed to fill them in on her situation, and her worry about what was next.

"I'm not sure yet. I guess I'll have to start over, find a job, and maybe get a roommate." Zoe cringed as she spoke, the thought of living with a stranger terrified her.

"You know, we've got a job opening," Scott and Grace said in unison.

"And a spare room," Grace added.

And for the first time in months, Zoe knew she was going to be just fine.

Kyoko Church

DIARY OF A LIBRARY NERD

That's what this will be. A safe haven.
A place for no holds barred ranting.
A place for secrets. And drawing. Even if it's bad. Even if it's wrong.
No one will see here. No one will see this.
This is just for me.

Charlotte has secrets.

Charlotte Campbell no longer recognizes her life. Once a shy, married librarian, she now finds herself jilted, holed up in her deceased father's run down cottage, and demoted to working in "The Dungeon" with only an automated book sorter for company. Then there's the drawings she does. They are not what her work colleagues might expect. And there's Nathan, a young patron at the library—the reason for her demotion and the inspiration for her art.

When Nathan's emails reveal a startling truth, Charlotte discovers a new dimension of her sexuality. But unsettling dreams from her past continue to plague her and Charlotte is eventually forced to confront her most deeply rooted fears.

Part Bridget Jones' Diary and part Story of O, Diary of a Library Nerd is the Wimpy Kid for adults. Compelling, erotic and accompanied by the drawings from Charlotte Campbell's very grown-up mind, this private memoir of exploration and discovery is not to be missed!